A HOUSE IN THE DARK
And Other Stories

A House In The Dark And Other Stories

By

Labo Yari

Fourth Dimension Publishing Co., Ltd.

First Published 1985 by
FOURTH DIMENSION PUBLISHING CO., LTD
16 Fifth Avenue, City Layout. PMB. 01164, Enugu, Nigeria.
Tel+234-42-459969. Fax+234-42-456904.
email: fdpbooks@aol.com, fdpbooks@yahoo.com
Web site: http://www.fdpbooks.com.

Reprinted 2002

ISBN 978-156-148-3

CONDITIONS OF SALE

Photoset and printed in Nigeria by
Fourth Dimension Publishers, Enugu.

CONTENTS

CONTENTS

THE DROUGHT

Darkness fell slowly, sliding across the few thorny trees, finally reaching the black ridges of the flatland.

It was another hard year. The harvest was not good because the rain was little. The peasants hoped for more rain, then prayed for it to come, but only scorching sun and dry wind came. The cattle became scraggy due to lack of grass, and people resorted to feeding their goats and sheep with tree leaves. The retreatment of peasants which began last year continued to rise.

Bello, with a broken axe slung over his shoulder, and carrying a small bundle of sticks, which was all the fire-wood he got after searching extensively in the arid land, was returning to his farm-stead. Earlier in the day, dressed with an over-patched jumper over a leather loin-cloth with no shoes, he had gone to Garu hamlet to visit his mother-in-law and to find out about his brother-in-law, Musa, from whom he had not heard for some months.

"Musa moved to town last month. He has already got a job from some people who are building roads all over the town," his mother-in-law told him.

Bello looked at the tall old woman of over sixty, dressed neatly in cotton-print and said, "Really? Has he moved with his wife and children?"

"Yes. Don't you see there are no children running about?" his mother-in-law asked, looking at him with surprise.

Bello was silent for a while as he sat on the straw mat which she had spread for him. He

1

thought of what he and Musa had discussed some months ago. They had promised, at the peak of the peasants' drift to towns, that they would stay on their farms believing the drought would not be severe and long.

"What do you think about the people rushing to town?" was the way Bello had started the discussion with Musa.

Musa gazed at him; after some moments he spoke.

"I was born and raised on the land and with the land I will remain. To go to town, to do what? Don't mind them, they will come back. I suppose those people in towns and cities eat. Well, if they do, what will they eat if we don't farm? They can't eat money, they need grain. Peasants are just being impatient, rain will come next season. After all, Allah will not abandon us. What have we done to Him?"

"You are perfectly right, Musa. We will cherish what we have, live by it, die by it," responded Bello, bringing the discussion to an end.

But since then Bello had sold all his goats and sheep to buy corn after he had exhausted his granary.

"Is something the matter?" his mother-in-law asked, cutting the chain of his thoughts. She handed him a small calabash full of watery porridge. After satisfying himself he sighed and replied: "I was just musing about."

"I really miss the children, but with the condition as it is, it is better for them to move," his mother-in-law began. She looked at the hem of her wrapper and continued, "Are you planning to move to town? If you are not, you better think about it. I do not see

2

the end of this drought. You are young and strong. Moreover, you and your wife have adult education certificates. The opportunities will be many for you."

"Our certificates are meant to help us in farming," he remarked.

"But you can't farm now. Not with this drought."

"Musa and I promised to stay on our farms come what may."

"That was rather too much and fatalistic."

"We feel it is necessary," he went on disregarding her remarks, "because we were born and raised on the farms. Just because there is a drought, it does not mean we give up. This is not the first drought. Our forebears endured and survived many droughts, why not us, then?"

"I insisted that Musa move, because it would be foolish of him to stay and suffer. He is not alone, he has three children and a wife. Gradually people will have to abandon this area whether they like it or not," his mother-in-law persisted. She looked at Bello and wondered why he could not see her point.

There was silence.

"I have never seen a drought like this," she said, scratching her head.

"I doubt if your forebears ever experienced a calamity like this. See how cattle are dying. Bello, your ancestors had no alternative but you have many. In the olden times the wishes of the people were not numerous. Also the population was small. Moreover, in the olden days each farmer cultivated enough for his family and the wives spun clothes, but not now. Go and live elsewhere, have a new life.

3

If you stay and suffer it is your own foolhardiness. You are not in chains and you cannot make rain."

Bello only listened as his mother-in-law talked on and on to convince him. But due to his fatalistic taste he refused to see the sense of what the old woman was saying. When she realised she was not convincing him, she became worried if not for Bello for her daughter.

When Bello left home that morning, his wife, Tadare normally had not returned from fetching water. She left home at dawn and returned with a pot of muddy water in the middle of the day. She trekked for a long distance in order to get the muddy water, for the few wells in the vicinity had dried up long ago and the women in the neighbourhood had to troop to a well on the way to town.

As soon as she returned home, she carried a calabash full of wild fruits, which she had plucked the previous afternoon, to the village square, where she sold it to children, with some luck. From the proceeds of the fruits she bought something edible. On her way back she picked up some cow dung to supplement her fire-wood.

As Bello approached his farm-stead that evening he began to smell dumplings. He sniffed, thinking his sense of smell was playing a trick on him for he was sure his wife could not cook dumplings, since there was no grain in the farm-stead. He had forgotten when he had tasted dumplings last. As soon as he dropped the fire-wood in front of his dwelling house, he shouted: "Tadare, I can smell dumplings!"

"By Allah and His Prophet, I am cooking it today. And not of corn or millet, but of the best

4

rice," Tadare said to her husband in high spirits. He came and gazed, unbelievably, as the steam of dumplings assailed him.

"How did you get rice in this hard time?"

"My brother gave me."

"Musa?"

"Yes, I saw him when I was returning to the farm from the well. He was coming from town riding a pillion on a motorcycle. He gave me two packets of rice and one of sugar. He sent his greetings and promised to come and see you tomorrow."

In the night, after they had eaten a good dinner, Bello told his wife about his visit to her mother. He narrated how she had tried to convince him to move out of his farm and settle in town.

"I really don't intend to move come what may," he said, fortifying his fatalistic taste. "I cherish my farm, for that is all I have. I will die defending it even against the drought. Now your brother is coming tomorrow, perhaps he will try to persuade me to move to town through you. Well, you hear my intention."

"It is all right for me, whatever you think is best for us. I myself don't really fancy living in a town. I am a country woman; I will never feel at home in a town. The drought will surely end and the fields will pulsate with greenery and the farms will blossom with corn," she responded to her husband.

Tadare loved her husband so very much that, at times, her mother and brother felt frightened. What with so many people wishing to marry her, with her tall and beautiful figure, yet she had turned them down and clung to a short and ugly man. They were married five years ago but had no child and she was

5

not worried, although she knew there was nothing her mother wished to see as much as a grand child from her only daughter.

Early the following morning Musa came to Bello's farm on a bicycle. His sister, for once, did not go to get water from the well in order to receive him.

"So you've betrayed me, and you moved without even telling me. You have become a fool, by abandoning farming. You are now a wage-earner, simply because the rains did not come. What will you do when the rains come next season? Will you return shamefacedly?" Bello asked, descending on Musa from his height of stubbornness.

"It is not that, Bello," Musa began defensively. "I have to face reality. From all signs it does not look as if it will rain enough in this area. As you can see the desert is already encroaching. I believe mother must have told you that she insisted I move to town. I am here today to tell you that I have already secured a job for you. Start to pack and let us go to town today. You can stay in my place until you are able to get yours."

Bello looked at Musa from top to bottom and was about to talk when his wife spoke.

"Thank you for the help, but we are not moving out of this place. Bello is right, there is no cause for alarm. Rain will certainly come next season. And we can manage with the little food stuff we have."

"Well, you have heard what your sister said. We can think for ourselves. We will stay here and that is all," Bello said, with an air of finality.

Musa realised that there was a kind of fatalistic taste acquired by his sister and her husband. He decided to do nothing believing that if things got worse, they would find their way to town without anybody's help. He bid farewell to them and returned to town.

From then onwards whenever Musa visited his mother, he stopped by at Bello's farm and gave them a few food stuffs without attempting to persuade Bello to move out of his farm.

Another rainy season found Bello with new hopes that the rains would be plenty to compensate for last season's failure. However, with every passing day, the signs of rain dwindled, as the wind became drier and the sun hotter. Gradually, the sun baked the earth, the scraggy cattle stripped the fields of every available blade of grass; the camels and goats ate the thorny shrubs, and the wind carried away the top fertile soil of the farms. The few farmers who remained adamant in their farms abandoned them and retreated to towns. But Bello and his wife remained on their farm refusing to move out in spite of pleas from his friends and mother-in-law. His hope for rain became stronger every day until it turned into a faith. And the faith gradually transformed into an illusion. He began to see clouds in an azure sky. The sound of nocturnal birds became that of thunder in his ears and the distant sun-rays looked like rain to him.

Tadare noticed the changes overcoming her husband. When she tried to talk to him to face reality, he felt annoyed. His annoyance frightened her, and from then onwards she agreed with whatever he told her and behaved as he wished though she knew it was strange.

"Oh merciful Allah! My child with that mad

7

man," Musa's mother said to her son after her repeated visits to Bello's farm all in efforts to persuade her daughter to leave her husband.

"He does not recognise me any more. He says I am a witch, who wants to set his farm on fire. And the poor child is believing him. She screams at me or says nothing to me. She now fetches water in the middle of the night. She too is turning mad. Please go and get her out of that farm, she may listen to you."

"After what I have heard of them I have not much hope. But I will go and try to see if I can persuade her to leave his house. As for him, his problem is beyond any human being. It is a pity a young and hard working man has become nutty." Musa replied to his mother before he left for Bello's farm.

Musa found Tadare alone, dressed in a wrapper with neither a blouse nor a head tie. When he came in she was sharpening hoes with a stone. She greeted him in a cool manner without lifting her head from her work.

"You look changed. What is the matter, sister?" Musa asked.

Tadare gave no answer to that.

"How is mama?" she inquired.

"She is all right, except she is terribly worried over your condition."

"Whose condition?"

"Yours."

There was silence.

"I am perfectly all right like any other normal person," she said.

"Well, how is your husband?"

8

"He is busy in the tillage."

Musa suppressed a smile, and addressed her. "What is he doing there at this time. Nobody is in the tillage now. Not with this drought. When are you leaving this place? In all the farm-steads I passed on my way here, I did not see anybody, even the goats are gone."

"You and mama always want us to abandon our farm, but we have already told you we are happy here. If it is because of the little help you send us, you can stop it. We will manage on our own," his sister said.

"I don't understand what is overcoming you. You used to be gentle and nice, but you now scream to mama."

Bello came in with a leather loin-cloth and a hoe slung over his shoulder.

"I am terribly busy with some weeds. They are trying to destroy my corn," Bello said to Musa.

Tadare looked at him and wanted to scream: "You are lying. And you know, you are lying," to her husband, but for certain reasons restrained herself. Bello selected another hoe and went out to the tillage.

"My sister," Musa began all over again. "I want to talk with you. You used to listen to me."

"What do you want to talk about?"

"About facing reality. About your husband and your inability to do something which is beyond your strength, not because you are a woman, no, because you are a human being."

"I do not understand."

"You will; Bello is mad. You know, but refuse to face it. No amount of your imagination or strength

9

can bring him back to sanity. It is better for you to face the bitter truth. After the initial shock you will recover. But if you refuse and cling to your imagination, one day he will mistake you for a log of wood. And he will hew you."

"Nonsense! Bello will never do that. He loves me. I will stay with him, he needs me."

"You will turn mad."

"That is what you hope."

"That is what mama and I are afraid of."

"I will go and help Bello. He is out alone in the tillage. Good-bye, greet mama," she said, walking out of the house.

Musa left the house in tears. As he walked away he saw his sister bending down beside her husband tilling the sandy ridges, as if there were plants.

"Did you hear the thunder yesterday night. No, you were snoring. I could not sleep, not with the way it rained, cat and dog. The harvest will surely be great this year," Bello said to his wife.

"Here we are again," she said to herself. "He is mad. It did not rain yesterday."

"What did your brother say?"

"He wants us to move out of here to town."

Bello laughed heartily, saying. "He is really jealous of my farm, seeing how the corn is growing. As for my groundnuts, no one in this district can do half of it. I don't know how many tons we will make this year. Don't you think we will harvest twice what we did last year?"

She kept silent. She knew what he said was false. There had been no harvest last year, though they had sowed the seeds. There was not a single cloud for months. The ridges were sandy, yet she was

10

behaving like him, tilling a farm where there was not a single blade of plant or grass.

"Has your brother brought me the cotton seeds? It is getting ready for sowing cotton seeds, you know."

"Yes they are in the house," she replied for fear of annoying him.

"Will they be enough?"

"More than enough."

"You don't believe me any more," he shouted, rising up.

Tadare looked into her husband's eyes and saw them very red and wild. He was really mad, she thought. She shuddered at the thought, but calmed herself so that he would not discover that she was afraid of him. She thought over what her brother had told her, but the possibility of Bello killing her mother if she deserted him, discouraged her from entertaining her brother's plea.

"Look!" shouted Bello, cutting her chain of thoughts. "It is going to rain. See how threatening the sky is." He kept gazing at the azure sky. Suddenly he screamed. "It is raining! Let us take cover in the house."

He threw his hoe and ran to the house, calling after his wife to follow him. She knew it was not raining. There was not the slightest sign of rain or that it would rain, but she ran after him as he commanded her.

In the night after Bello had slept, Tadare was thoughtful. She would soon go mad if she continued to stay with him, one part of her told her. Another part told her to stick to her imagination. But that was only for a while. Gradually, the idea that she was

not facing reality got a better part of her. She heard
Bello snoring. She wondered what he would do to
her when he woke up, for he was rapidly becoming
mad. Would he mistake her for a log of wood, as her
brother had said? Would he go and kill her mother if
she deserted him? Slowly her big hands found his
neck. Gently she squeezed. He struggled for breath,
she tightened her grasp. She kept her hands until she
was sure he was breathless. Then, with incredible
speed, she collected what she could. She walked out
of the farm-stead into the darkness. But before she
reached her mother's house, she was drenched to
her skin by a heavy downpour, like she had never
seen in her life-time.

HARD TO BE SOFT

Huzai, the daughter of the tanner, was walking briskly towards the corner of the alley with a plate of roasted groundnuts balanced on her head.

Fatahu, the son of the builder, was speeding on his bicycle towards the corner. In an attempt to avoid pushing her down he fell down from his bicycle. She arched forward in fright and her plate of roasted groundnuts fell down.

Rilwanu, Huzai's uncle, a lean never-do-well person of about forty-five was at the end of the alley when the accident happened. He walked to the scene as Fatahu got up, propped his bicycle against the wall and began helping Huzai to retrieve some of the groundnuts.

"My goodness, what are you going to do with those nuts? Half of them are pebbles. You won't sell them to your customers, would you? Unless you want to drive them away," Rilwanu remarked when he reached the scene.

"There aren't many pebbles. I will make sure I pick all of them out, uncle," Huzai responded.

"No, stop it! You are wasting your time. Here, that will make up for those nuts," Rilwanu said, giving her some coins.

Huzai received the coins without any surprise. It was typical of her uncle, though he never had enough. He was always coming to her father for money. And as soon as he got it he ended up in a gambling or a drinking house. He was always generous, especially when he was lucky with cards. So she knelt down and received the money, saying, "Thank you very much, uncle."

"Oh, it is all right," Rilwanu responded.

"I am sorry, sir. Thank you for coming to my aid," Fatahu expressed his gratitude.

"Come on, forget it. Aren't you the son of the builder of builders? I know you very well. Your father is my good friend. A real fine fellow. Never hurts a fly. Always helpful to his friend."

Huzai looked at Fatahu and smiled. Fatahu tried to speak, but could not form any words.

Rilwanu realised that his presence was embarrassing them. He turned to walk away and bumped into a man with a big belly and a wart on the top of his nose.

"Excuse me, I am sorry, Nuridini," Rilwanu lamented.

"Don't bother, I have been looking for you," Nuridini said, eyeing Huzai.

"Me, what for?" asked Rilwanu, "I have nothing to pawn."

"No, not on that. There is a favour I would like you to do for me."

Rilwanu became silent. He knew Nuridini was not only a miser but a wicked person. It was strongly rumoured that he had whipped his wife to death. And since then his children had been neglected. No women agreed to marry him in spite of his money.

"I'd rather do the favour here."

"By Allah, come! It is a small one."

"All right young ones, look after yourself. I am off with this miser," Rilwanu said to Huzai and Fatahu.

"I am sorry," Huzai and Fatahu said in unison after Rilwanu and Nuridini had gone.

14

They smiled.

"Well, let me give you the nuts I retrieved. They are okay, there are no pebbles in them," Huzai remarked.

"Oh, no! Thank you,"

"Oh sure! you should have it."

"Please don't mind."

"I like you to have them. It is a gift from me."

"In that case I will have them," he said, receiving the nuts.

After that he walked to his bicycle. He turned and smiled at her before he pedalled away.

The next time Huzai saw Fatahu was at a building site where he was helping to erect a house. He was sitting astride a wall. She stood by amazed as she watched him catching balls of mud with his left hand and moulding them skilfully into a wall with both of his hands. He was so absorbed in his work that he did not notice her until the thrower made a bad aim.

"What are you thinking about?" Fatahu reproached him.

"I want to ease myself. I am a bit pressed."

"Really? I thought you were reminding me of the break. Isn't it time for it?" Fatuhu remarked, jovially. They laughed and he climbed down.

He was washing his hands when he saw Huzai. For some moments he stood speechless.

"Well, well, how are you?" he asked, smiling and walking to her.

"I am all right," she responded, smiling.

"Thank you for those delicious nuts. I really enjoyed them."

"I am pleased to hear that."

15

"Where are you going?"

"I am going to my aunt's, she lives near by. I often come this way. It is strange I never saw you. I could not believe my eyes when I saw you on top of that wall receiving those balls. How many houses have you erected? You are really good at it."

"No, I am only helping my father. He is not here today. He has gone to another site. I am often reproached by him. He thinks I am still an apprentice. All the same, I am glad to hear that you're impressed."

"No, you are more than an apprentice. He is only being modest. I have seen many builders, but they cannot match you. You are really skilful. Let me not disturb you. Go and carry on with your work."

"You're not disturbing my work, Huzai. It is time for a break."

"Well, I really have to go. My aunt is expecting me. See you again."

"Wait, let me see," said Fatahu, putting his hand in his pocket. "Here, I really should have paid for those groundnuts I made you scatter."

"I am not receiving it if it is for payment of groundnuts. After all my uncle already paid for it."

"Then accept it as a gift."

"In that case, thank you," she said, receiving the money. She walked on, thinking of Fatahu.

"How does he know my name?" she kept asking herself without bothering to find the answer.

At home she handed over the amount given her by Fatahu to her mother and explained how she had met him.

"All the same who is he? I never heard of him," commented her mother.

16

"He is the son of the builder," said Huzai.

"There are many builders in the town. How come you did not know which of them? I don't want you to get involved with bad people. You know how strict your father is. He won't be happy to hear you receiving money from boys like that."

"Every girl does that."

"You are not every girl."

"Well, I don't think Fatahu will hurt me. He is more serious than most of the boys I know. Uncle Rilwanu may be able to know his father. You can ask him."

"I really don't think your uncle can differentiate between a good boy and a bad one."

"Fatahu is a good boy, mother. A look at his eyes will convince you. He is also going to be a famous builder."

"Who is going to be a famous builder?" Rilwanu cut in as he came into the house.

Both mother and daughter started because they did not hear his footsteps.

"Let her tell you," her mother said.

"Fatahu is going to be a famous builder, uncle. Don't you believe me?"

"He is already a famous builder. He has erected more than five houses."

"Well, did you hear, mother?"

"I am not interested in whether he is a famous builder or not. What interests me is whether he is a good boy or not. And how come you have received his money?"

"Lazzatu," Rilwanu addressed Huzai's mother. "Fatahu is the son of Mudassaru, the builder of builders. You cannot say you don't know him."

17

"All right, Huzai, you may go out to your sister's house. She has sent for you," Lazzatu said, dismissing her daughter.

After that she kept quiet for a while, thinking. She knew Mudassaru very well. He had been among her suitors, but because she dragged her feet he left her and she ended up marrying Huzai's father, Amadu. She had regretted it, but later accepted it as her fate.

"How good is the boy?" she asked at last.

"As good as his father. Never quarrels, always respects his elders and hardworking. Builders are already reckoning with him."

"But this idea of giving Huzai money, where will it lead to? I am afraid of it."

"Don't tell me you have already forgotten your girlhood. The boy simply fancies Huzai. She too fancies him. I could see from their eyes, so you better encourage her. Don't let her make your own mistake. Give her all the encouragement she needs."

"I don't regret marrying your brother," Lazzatus retorted.

"That's what you always say, but your face always betrays you. Everybody knows you are far from being happy. However, let us forget about that. Huzai and Fatahu are a good match. So all we should do is to encourage them."

"I agree with you they need our encouragement. All the same, you know your brother. He always makes a choice of husbands for his daughters. Suppose he plans to marry her to another man, won't it be cruel to Fatahu and her? That is my fear."

"If all hopes are doomed, fears might be duped,

18

Lazzatu. Let us hope your husband will agree to Fatahu marrying Huzai."

"Let us then cross our fingers and see what will happen," Lazzatu said.

And this was what happened in the next two to three years.

Huzai and Fatahu saw a lot of each other. They often met at her aunt's house. She continued to accept his gifts and always took them to her mother. Her relations both on paternal and maternal sides approved and encouraged her to marry Fatahu, who often visited them. However, her father was kept in the dark until one evening when Rilwanu informed him.

"The son of the builder of builders is madly in love with Huzai. I believe he won't rest until he marries her. They will make a perfect couple," Rilwanu told Amadu.

"Never heard of it," responded Amadu.

"You are now hearing it."

"I hope you are not receiving any money from him or any member of his family. If you are doing that, it will be your own headache."

"Though I am considered as a never-do-well, I have not reached that stage."

"You better not. I decide who marries my daughter."

"I am fully aware of that. Have I ever given off your daughter for marriage?"

"You dare not."

"I know, because I am penniless."

"Not that."

"What else, am I not your brother?"

"You are, but you hardly know the right man to

19

make a good husband. You married only once. And that lasted two months."

"All right that is enough."

As soon as Amadu came home that evening he called his wife and enquired about his daughter's relation to Fatahu.

"What is going on between Huzai and the son of the builder?"

"What have you heard, my dear?"

"Rilwanu was telling me that a sort of relationship has developed between them. If it is true, how come such things are going on behind my back?"

"It is true both of them like one another, but nobody from his family made any approach."

"They better not."

"Why, dear?"

"I have not yet decided who is going to marry my daughter."

"Then there is no reason why Fatahu and Huzai should be discouraged in their relationship."

"All right, leave it at that. Don't let me lose my temper."

Three months later, when Huzai was sixteen and Fatahu nineteen, his family made a formal approach through Amadu's sister, Marwa.

"My nephew has seen your daughter and wishes to ask for her hand in marriage. I believe you are the right person to come to," Fatahu's aunt said the day she led a group of elderly women to the house of Huzai's aunt.

"Truly, there is nothing I wish to see more than a marriage between the two. He is such a lovely boy. There is no doubt they are in love. If it is within my power, I will give you an affirmative reply. I need the

20

consent of her mother and father. All be it, I promise I will do my best."

The following day Marwa went to see her brother on the matter. First she went to the girl's mother.

"I will be glad to see them married. But you know how your brother is. You have to approach him tactfully. He is at work," Lazzatu said to Marwa.

"There is something I wish to discuss with you," Marwa said to her brother after the usual salutations.

"What is it?"

"The family of the builder's son approached me soliciting you for the hand of Huzai for their son."

"Rejected."

"Oh, no!"

"Why not? Do you want to force me to marry off my daughter? You know you cannot do that."

"I cannot," she uttered, swallowing the lump in her throat. "That is why I came to you, brother."

"Well, tell them I am not ready to give their son my daughter. In fact I have already promised someone. And she'll soon be married."

"Who is he?"

"Nuridini, the merchant."

"You don't mean it!"

"Huzai is my daughter."

"Truly, but is that not going too far?"

"Well, I can give her off for marriage to whomever I like."

"Does she know?"

"She will know."

"But she is in love with Fatahu."

"So what?"

21

"You will not change your mind for the future and well-being of your daughter?"

"Not for the son of the builder."

"Not even for me and her mother."

"Not for anybody."

"Then there is no need for further discussion."

Marwa could not form the words when she went to tell Lazzatu of her unsuccessful mission.

"He did not agree with the idea?" Lazzatu asked.

"He is giving her to Nuridini, the merchant." Marwa said in tears.

Lazzatu fell silent.

"I am sorry. It is painful. It will pain Fatahu and Huzai most. Damn my cruel brother!" Marwa exclaimed.

She delayed conveying the bad news to Fatahu's family, hoping that her brother would change his mind. However, Fatahu heard the news from Huzai.

"Our hopes are shattered," Huzai told him in tears. "My father said I will marry Nuridini."

"You don't mean it! He is not only older than your father, but a miser, dirty and cruel. In fact no woman agrees to marry him, not after what he did to his late wife."

"With all that I am going to marry him. And the marriage will take place very soon. My mother has been weeping since the day my father told her his intention. What can we do, Fatahu? I love you."

"I love you too, Huzai. I want to marry you. I want you to be the mother of my children. And now ..." He paused, feeling a lump in his throat.

A few days later Fatahu came up with what they could do.

22

"Let us run away, Huzai. Let us go and settle in another town far away from them, where they will never hear of us. Far away, where we can marry and bring up children. I don't mind learning another trade. We could go even in the middle of the forest, build huts, clear the bush, cultivate the land. Live among the birds and animals. Yes, let us do that in the name of love."

"Oh, that will be marvelous! How I love you! And how I hate Nuridini!" Huzai exclaimed. "But all the same, I cannot elope with you. I am my father's daughter. I have to listen to my father and do as he says. He wants me to marry Nuridini. I don't want it, my mother hates the idea and nobody in my family likes the marriage. But a man is the master of his family. I know marrying Nuridini may lead me to torments and possibly to my death. But since my father wants it, I must obey him. I will marry Nuridini."

On the day the marriage contract between Huzai and Nuridini was to be entered, Rilwanu had a lucky day on gambling. Consequently he had his fill in the drinking house before coming to the ceremony. As a brother to Huzai's father, custom demanded that the ceremony took place in his house. But as he had no permanent abode, it was decided that his mere presence was enough.

When he arrived for the ceremony at his brother's house he found the house in a state of brawl. Lazzatu and her daughter were roaring for mercy from Amadu not to allow the ceremony to go on. Amadu's sister was also pleading with him to consider his stand.

"This is not a day of grief. It is a day for

23

merriment. Cheer up ladies," Rilwanu said in a drawl.

"Hear it, my brother is agreeing with me. Cheer them up, Rilwanu," Amadu retorted.

"Who the hell are you talking to?" asked Rilwanu.

"Oh, are you not on my side?"

"Whose side? Listen, I am disgusted with the whole affair. You are so inhuman that you don't care about the feelings of your own daughter or her mother. What are you trying to be, Amadu? It is true I gamble and drink, but that does not stop me from seeing things in their right places."

"Now, now, now, Rilwanu. Don't go too far, stop it. You are drunk, go and sleep. Don't come and disgrace me on a day like this," Amadu said.

"Amadu, are you talking to me like that? Whatever I am doing I am your elder brother. Moreover, the issue at stake has nothing to do with my drinking. You may not drink, but you are worst than alcoholic and ..."

"Get out of my house," Amadu shouted.

"I am not and if you don't be careful, I will slap you. Everybody in this town knows Nuridini. He whipped his wife to death. He is a miser and a cruel man. For over three years he has been trying to marry, but no woman agrees to marry him. He even tried to marry prostitutes and invalids without success, and now you are trying to marry your own daughter to him. It means you hate her and her mother because you fully know they are both agonised by the idea."

"No, stop it Rilwanu, I don't hate them."

"Then why are you going to marry her off to Nuridini?"

24

"He loves her."

"But she does not love him."

"That is not necessary. He will look after her well since he loves her."

"No, I tell you why you are marrying her off to him. He gave you money, but your daughter is not a slave. You cannot sell her to a man who may kill her."

"Come on, brother, he will not kill her."

"She will never be happy with him."

"Happiness is not the purpose of marriage."

"Ah, I got it. You want to saddle her with problems as you did to her mother. You know the girl does not love Nuridini; she loves Fatahu. But you are not going to marry her off to Fatahu because his father was the man your wife wanted to marry. She is regretting marrying you. Fatahu's father is better than you. You could not be like him, an understandable person. Now you want to transfer your hatred to his son, isn't it? You are out of your mind, Amadu. You have no moral right to ruin the future of your daughter. She is not going to marry Nuridini. After all I am your brother and Marwa is our sister. The two of us have agreed to rescind your decision."

Rilwanu turned to his sister and asked. "Do you agree with my decision?"

Marwa nodded in agreement.

"Well, Amadu, your brother and sister have rescinded your decision. What have you got to say?"

There was silence for some moments.

"I have accepted your decision," Amadu said.

"Now you are really being my little brother," said

25

Rilwanu, smiling. He turned to his sister and spoke, "Sister, I am convinced that Huzai and Fatahu will make an ideal couple. They love each other. They are young. Our permitting them to marry will make them happy. And there is nothing I like more as making her happy. So I am seeking your approval and that of my younger brother in giving Huzai's hand to Fatahu."

"Permission granted," Marwa and Amadu replied in unison.

CAVALIER OF THE PLAIN

As I approach the hamlet, which amounts to no
more than a few hovels of dried mud, the sun begins
to set. The day has been very hot, stifling hot. My
horse is very tired, foam drips from his mouth and
his nostrils flare amidst a swarm of flies.

I have ridden through the plain for the whole day;
peasants pausing in their work, saluting me in the
the familiar manner. I have been riding from
hamlets to villages, from villages to towns for over
one year. I no longer have a home. I am on the road.
I sleep wherever night catches up with me, be it
among the people or in the open. I have no problem
of food or fodder. Some people give me money
while others give me kolanuts. I always carry one or
two roasted chicken's legs in my haversack in case I
find no food. My bedding, a spare gown and
trousers serve as a cushion on my saddle.

I am content now with roaming in the plain of
Hausaland, although I was once the favourite
groom of the chief of my village.

And yet I am beginning to feel the stabs of regret,
for thoughts of Safiya come back to my mind again.

Safiya had been dead for more than three years,
and now my memories of her were beginning to
surprise me.

It was a day like this. I was coming to the hamlet
on a pleasure ride. I was riding the chief's white
stallion. He was cotton white, with black, luminous
eyes. I groomed his mane perfectly on that day.

I was attired in a white gown over a black woven
one with a pair of loose trousers, which had red silk
embroidery from knees to ankles. I was turbanned

27

in black silk, while my sword, in its famous Kano-Leather scabbard with a tasselled sword-sling of silk, was hanging on my left.

A group of women, carrying water-pots, caught my attention as they stood admiring me. To impress them more, I gave a slight touch to the stirrups and the stallion bolted forward, as the women held their noses, making a thrill noise, in unison. As I charged forward, I saw the scribe sitting among some people in front of his house. Suddenly, I drew my sword from the scabbard. With a hair-raising cry, I spurred the stallion and he ran full tilt. Within a little distance from the scribe, I pulled the reins and the stallion backed up and jerked from side to side in protest. Amidst laughter and admiration, I dismounted.

The scribe saluted me, feeling excited by my display. One did such a display only for chiefs. No wonder, the scribe received me as an equal, civility for civility, though he knew I was a groom. After some moments he sent for drinking water for me. To my amazement, the woman who brought the water was among the group of women carrying water-pots, who were actually the cause of the special feat I had performed. Safiya, as I learnt her name later, knelt down and gave me the water in a well decorated calabash. I drank a lot and left a little in which I put some beautiful kolanuts and some coins, which I brought out from the huge pocket of my white gown. Safiya received the calabash, smiling. The cause of my generous gesture was the belief that with the performance I had made, the scribe would certainly not let me go back to my village without giving me some money.

However, my gesture aroused a passionate feeling in Safiya. The passion that threw her across my path would take possession of her with a peculiar strength she had never known.

Safiya was the niece of the scribe. She was recently divorced. However, her husband divorced her only once, not thrice as was the custom with the muslims, so there was the possibility of reconciliation with her husband. People were already saying that she was depending on that idea, that was why she came to stay with the scribe who could use his influence on her husband. The husband was a well-known hunter in the hamlet and getting wives was not a problem for him. In fact he had already married two more wives after Safiya had left his house. But with all his numerous marriages, he never had a child.

The three wives of the scribe were happy to have Safiya staying with them, for she helped them in many ways. The eldest wife, Binta, showed more interest in her. She made her sleep in her hut, though Safiya had her small bundle in the hut given to her by the scribe. The hut was in the first courtyard, which was separated from the huts of the wives with a cornstalk wall. Binta sent Safiya on some special errands to leather workers. Nobody knew the nature of the errands, though the other two wives of the scribe frowned and joked about the errands. Now they were happy when Safiya went in raptures over me and the stallion, especially when they noticed the coldness with which Binta perceived Safiya's raptures.

Safiya had no beauty, but was young and childless. The first time I visited her I realised that it was only when I was drunk that I could love her, so I made a point to visit her with my small gourd of cornwine, which I always picked free of charge, from the house of the chief of Maguzawa near our village.

The scribe encouraged me to cultivate the friendship with his niece. And as soon as he noticed that we were in love, either through indolence or some vice, he ignored us, after he had made her move to the hut he had given her in the courtyard.

When I entered Safiya's hut for the first time I was amazed at the neatness of the place. I noticed a type of leather rod on her bed. I had never seen its kind before, and I was about to ask her when I saw her hiding it nervously.

"You are a prince on a horse. I am happy to be with you," she said, after she had hid the rod.

"Has your husband never ridden a horse?" I asked, looking at her.

"What, are you jealous?" she smiled.

"Does it change anything? After all you still see him. When are you going back to him?"

"Forget about him. He will not stand in our way to happiness," she said, brushing the back of her hand across her forehead.

"But he only divorced you once not thrice. And don't tell me he stops sending you gifts on market days," I reminded her.

"I never received anything from any man since the day you gave me that present. I will never betray you," she said, welcoming me into her arms.

The memory of her serious, pathetic and blissful look as she received me into her arms infuriated me. When I woke up at dawn, on her cornstalk bed, which had no more than three straw-mats, the cool morning air was drifting in through the thatch of the hut and the birds were singing. My blood was charged up and I felt in high spirits. She woke up, went to the well and returned with water for my bath. After I washed myself, she brought me her calabash of porridge from which I satisfied my hunger. I picked the best of the kolanuts from a tin she pushed to me and chewed them noisily.

It was then I began to think that I should have been alone or on a horse back. I was enraged with the small amount of tenderness she got from me. The rage that arose in me mounted as if step by step, and with each step my anguish widened and took on a greater variety of shades. She noticed it, but went along with rearranging her dishes and calabashes blissfully.

Through my visits to Safiya's hut, I noticed the intensity of Binta's anger. She did not only cut off her usual gifts to me but stopped acknowledging my greetings.

"Nobody will stand in our way. Don't mind them," Safiya said to me the day I refused to spend the night in her hut after I found her and Binta together and behaving strangely.

"You better get it out of your feeble mind that you mean anything to me," I shouted at her.

"Don't you love me?" she asked, softly.

"The little I have, I burned on horses."

"But we are still good friends, aren't we?" she inquired, smiling forcibly.

"Listen, your hypocrisy worries me so much. You have many lovers. You and me are only two people who get on well in bed, and that is all."

"Him!" She exclaimed, grabbing my gown.

I went into her hut, but she had a horrible time during my stay.

"Have you ever married?" she asked me after I sat on her bed.

"Yes."

"What happened to her?"

"I murdered her." I went on describing in the most grotesque way, how I murdered my wife. But all were figments of my mind, for I had never married. Safiya kept looking at me in horror and after I finished my story said, "Why did you do it?"

"I met her with a woman." I replied.

Safiya began to breathe heavily. I thought she was going to break my head with one of her dishes.

"And did you love her?" she asked at last.

"Yes," I replied.

From that day I never saw Binta in Safiya's hut. As to her husband she told me she would never go back.

At times when trying to shake off the feeling of distress that assailed me whenever I remembered the sight of the leather rod I saw on Safiya's bed, I would run, bridle and saddle the stallion. In a single moment, without any constraint from my body, I would mount the stallion, my limbs falling into their true balance and I would become another man.

As soon as I mounted the stallion, I would grasp the reins in my hands and, without ever getting a hint from the spurs, the stallion would back up and jerk until he stood on his hind legs. I would hold him there until he began to lose his balance. Then I would gradually slacken the reins and let him come down. In a flash, I would give him a touch of the

32

spurs and he would hurl forward. He would run and run in the plain, the wind tearing at my face until my eyes filled with water.

But the moment I pulled the reins and the stallion stopped, my ordeal would begin again. It was after that, that I realized whatever I did when the frenzy passed, I would return to what I was.

One night we were sitting in her hut when Safiya suddenly looked at me with a start.

"Can you marry me?" she asked.

"Yes," I replied nonchalantly.

"Do you love me?"

"I really don't know."

"How would you feel if I died tomorrow?"

"How would I know?"

"What about if I go to another man?"

"People always betray one another, if that's what you mean."

"Suppose I return to my husband."

"Didn't I hear that he has four wives?"

"He came here yesterday. He brought me some birds."

"Really?"

"Yes."

"You can go and be his concubine."

"No, not even a wife. There is no point. He is not a man," she said, sadly. I looked at her, she smiled pathetically, adding, "I have a new lover."

I did not say anything to that. But that night, when I lay on her bed, I felt I was immersed in anguish. Who was this ugly woman? Why was she worrying my life? Why could I not escape from her? I cursed the impulse which led me to pity her. Why should I be associating myself with her? What did I

33

derive from my association with her? I left her bed. I was dressing in the dark when I heard her voice.

"Why are you trying to sneak out? There is no need for that. Good night, if you are going."

I felt like a wanted man who had been found hiding in a dark corner. I walked out of her hut and knelt down easing myself, when she came out, believing I had gone, and went into Binta's hut. My thoughts went back to the leather rod. I feel a pang in my stomach. I left the house quickly, grinding my teeth in order not to cry.

After that event Safiya came to my village several times looking for me. Each time she came I hid from her.

The scribe sent for me, I refused to come and see him.

Then one night desire got the better part of me. I bridled and saddled my horse. It was only a short distance from my village to the hamlet, so I decided to trot it.

Before I dismounted from my horse, in front of the scribe's house, a voice came piercing the darkness.

"If you have come for Safiya she is dead. She was found hanging from a tree," the scribe said with bitterness. I sat on my horse shaking.

THE TENACIOUS LADY

Jide, a little cheerful girl, brought out some stones from a tin. Her mother, Lucy Idahaso, and her younger brother, Iriabe watched her as she counted the stones aloud.

"Thirty," she said, dropping the last stone. "Today is thirty days since Daddy has gone away and he will stay there for three years. Who will be feeding us? Who will be paying our school fees? My God, maybe we have to stop going to school."

"Stop it, Jide!" shouted her mother. "You will make it worse for us. Go and wash and come to go to school."

"But Mummy," Iriabe complained, "I don't want to go to school any more. Last week my classmates were saying my father was in prison. Is it true? You said Daddy had gone overseas."

"Your Daddy has travelled, Iriabe. Don't mind your classmates," Lucy Idahaso said to her son.

"They are not lying. My playmate told me that my father had stolen some money. Did Daddy steal?"

"Go and wash," commanded Lucy Idahaso, climbing down from her bed.

Jide and Iriabe ran out of the shack into the dirty courtyard.

Lucy Idahaso came out of the shack and went in to the shanty kitchen. She roasted bananas for breakfast. She did not fry them because there was no oil. She also made porridge.

She served the breakfast fully dressed. She had the basket with which she would go to the market to

35

buy fruits, which she would sell in front of her house.

"We're going to the museum today. Can you give me a shilling, Mummy?" Iriabe asked, dressing into his brown khaki shirt and shorts.

"A shilling," said his mother unhappily. "You got your pocket-money day before yesterday."

"You don't call a shilling pocket-money. Daddy used to give me five shillings pocket-money," Iriabe replied, putting his school box on his head.

That rebuffed her for a moment. She made an effort and said, "Don't you see your Daddy is away?"

"Where has he gone? You said he is not in prison. You don't tell me where he is," her son responded with an air of defiance.

"I'll tell you when you come back from the school," she said, in a faltering voice.

"That's what you always say. Keep your lousy shilling," Iriabe replied, going out of the room followed by his elder sister.

After her children had gone to school, Lucy Idahaso, slim, about thirty was overwhelmed by a sense of sadness and melancholy. She looked around her shack. She saw her delicate, serious, almost severe face in the small mirror hanging on the wall.

"Where is my life going?" she asked herself.

She remembered her husband. A tall, sombre man with light features, shy and withdrawn to himself.

She had met Garuba Idahaso in Benin when she was a teenager. She was then living in her uncle's house because her parents died when she was a little girl. Garuba Idahaso was living near her. They became friends easily and remained so. He taught her to read and write because she did not go to school.

After his secondary education, he secured a clerical job with the United African Company in Benin. He worked for three years to save for the bride price. They married according to Benin tradition.

A year after they married, Garuba Idahaso secured a better job with the government in Lagos. Three months after their arrival in Lagos, Jide was born, and three years later Iriabe was born.

Most of their friends in Lagos were from their hometown. Among them was David Borha, a tall, good-looking bachelor, who had been Garuba Idahaso's classmate at the secondary school. Unlike Garuba Idahaso, David Borha was well off. He had inherited a lot of money from his rich father who had died recently.

One Friday afternoon, Lucy Idahaso was selling fruits when David Borha came in his new Peugeot.

"Lucy, your husband is in the police station, you better come with me," David Borha had said to her when he came out of the car.

"What?" she asked.

An immense fear opened like an abyss before her eyes.

"He's got mixed up in a dirty case. He needs someone to bail him. Don't worry, things will be all right," David Borha said, consoling her.

On their way to the police station, she scarcely saw the people in the street. As far as she was

37

concerned she might have been passing through a deserted city in the middle of the night.

"Somebody wants to put me into trouble," her husband said to her when he saw her.

David Borha bailed him out and drove them to their home. After their children had gone to bed that night, Lucy Idahaso asked her husband what had really happened.

"I was returning home from the ministry," her husband began. "A man came to me at the bus stop. He introduced himself to me as Isaka Ayo. He said he had met me at David's party. His face was familiar to me.

"He was carrying a box in one hand and a brief-case in the other. He asked me to hold his brief-case for him to buy a cigarette.

"I saw nothing wrong in that, so I agreed. As soon as he disappeared in the crowd, a policeman came."

Motionless and spell-bound, his wife looked at him.

"The policeman asked me whether the brief-case was mine. I told him a friend asked me to hold it for him to buy a cigarette. The policeman waited, saying he would like to see the owner.

"'Would you mind coming to the station with me, Oga?' the policeman said, when Isaka Ayo did not return after five minutes.

"'On what charge?' I asked the policeman.

"'No charge, Oga, only for further enquiries. That brief-case looks like the one which was snatched a few minutes ago.'

"I followed him, realising a refusal would not be in my own interest.

38

"At the station I related how Isaka Ayo came and asked me to hold the brief-case for him. They called David Borha, who told them he did not know Isaka Ayo. The owner of the brief-case said I looked like the man who had snatched the brief-case."

"What did they find in the brief-case?" his wife asked.

"There were two hundred pounds in notes and two wrist watches," he replied.

He looked at his wife.

"Do you believe me?" he asked, searching her eyes for approval.

"Yes, I do," she said.

Then with a promptitude that seemed hardly credible she threw her arms around him.

"Let's forget it. Things will be all right. Truth will prevail," she murmured.

A week later when Garuba Idahaso went to his office, he found a letter of dismissal on his table. He went to his boss and protested.

"There's nothing I can do, Garuba Idahaso," his boss began. "The police reported what you did yesterday."

"But until I'm proved guilty, nobody should conclude that I am a thief," replied Garuba Idahaso, slamming the door.

The case went to court and Garuba Idahaso was sentenced to three years' imprisonment with hard labour.

One evening, Lucy Idahaso was sitting in her shack and her children were sleeping when David Borha visited her.

"What are you going to do now?" David Borha asked her after he sat down.

"Just wait. I know it will be difficult to wait for three years. However, where can I go with two children? All will come to him who waits, isn't it?" she replied, looking at him.

"Sometimes a little never comes to him who waits, Lucy. It will be unwise for you to wait. You need money and a man. You can come and live with me. I'm not married," David Borha said.

There was silence.

"To live with you in sin," she said, after this significant silence.

"But you did not marry in the church," David Borha responded.

"Is it not a bit treacherous of you? I thought you were a good friend of my husband. Is the friendship gone to pieces because he is in jail?"

"I don't mean that."

"Look Mr. Borha, I'm no longer a little girl, neither a loose woman," she said in the ironical malevolent voice of one who wants to fight. "I'm now a woman who has gone through many things, who has had sorrow. Oh yes, this is not the first."

Her body began to palpitate.

"I have been through many troubles and many difficulties, but nevertheless, I had never succumbed to the whims of material things. You see, I always preserve my dignity."

"I don't mean to insult you. I was merely joking," replied David Borha, when he realised the irritation and disgust, the pitiful storm with which his offer was rejected.

"You joke a lot, David," she said.

Sleep did not come to Lucy Idahaso easily that night. Why did she refuse David Borha's offer, she

40

asked herself. Could she wait for three years? She remembered that David Borha said she needed a man. That could as well mean that she could get another man, not necessarily her husband's friend.

Why should she leave her husband, another part of herself said. Even if she could get another man, who never knew her husband, would virtue not turn him to be a wicked man. It also seemed to her, owing to her moral obligation to her children, that waiting for her husband was the only epilogue her life deserved.

"After all, life does not change. It refuses to change," she said to herself fortifying her fatalistic taste.

Then she remembered that her husband had a good land in Benin.

"I'll go and sell it. I'll use the money to maintain my children until my husband is released," she consoled herself.

Suddenly, she remembered it was already noon. She picked her basket and hurriedly went out of the house for market.

In the evening, after a frugal dinner, Lucy Idahaso called her daughter, who was playing with other children in the courtyard.

"Jide, I'll be going to Benin tomorrow morning. I'll come back in the evening. Look after your brother," she said to her daughter.

"All right, Mummy," the daughter replied.

"What are you going to do in Benin?" asked Iriabe, who was sitting near his mother.

"I'm going to get some money," she responded to her son.

41

"Did Daddy not leave some for you?" Iriabe inquired.

"He left some, but I need more."

Early, the following morning, Lucy Idahaso took all the money she had. She went to the motor park where she took a bus to Benin. When she arrived in Benin she went to the house of her husband's uncle, Odeh Ikwele.

"It is not possible to sell that land without a written permission from your husband," Odeh Ikwele explained to her, when she told him the purpose of her visit.

"He's in prison. I can't visit him. I can't face him in that uniform," she said, sadly.

"Don't be childish. Go, he will be glad to see you," Odeh Ikwele advised her.

He gave her money for her return fare to Lagos, when he found she had no money.

She arrived late in Lagos, and found her children sleeping.

She was preparing to go to bed when she heard a knock on the door.

"Who is it?" she asked.

"It is David."

Lucy Idahaso hesitated for a moment, then she opened the door saying to herself, "what will happen will happen."

"I hope I am not disturbing you. I came to see whether there is any help I can render," David Borha said, sitting down in the poorly lit shack.

"I'll tell him of my financial problem. I'll tell him I went to Benin today and returned penniless," one part of herself said.

But she did not.

42

"You are very kind, David Borha, but I have no immediate problem. I'll tell you whenever I need your help," she replied, carefully articulating her syllables.

David Borha felt happy. He brought out a cigarette case from his pocket. He took one and lit it with his golden lighter.

Lucy Idahaso remained for a moment deep in thought, but without any sign of sadness or embarrassment.

"Tonight is the time," David Borha thought. His fixed motionless gaze ignored the children, who were sleeping on the floor. Desire gave him vision: Lucy Idahaso sitting down entirely naked on the bed. He seemed to see her firm body, shining and trembling for desire, and her small buttocks quivering to increasing excitement and she clinging to him as if she would never let him go.

"How is work?" Lucy Idahaso said, shattering his fantasy.

"Oh, as usual. Nothing extraordinary," he replied, making an effort to appear cool and calm.

Lucy Idahaso began to see the gloom inside her shack increasing. It engulfed the iron-sheet walls and the few objects in the shack. It grew thicker and thicker, descending upon her children and David Borha. The light flickered and grew darker and, finally, the solitary bulb hanging from the ceiling went off.

"What's the matter?" Lucy Idahaso said, feeling shrouded with no hope to escape from the impenetrable darkness and David Borha.

"It's NEPA, the usual thing," David Borha replied.

43

"Now is the moment," he thought.

Lucy Idahaso felt a hand on her lap. She shivered, but made no effort to resist.

"I'll let him have what he wants. Men are always like that. They won't stop until they get what they want. After all what can I do. What will happen will happen," she thought.

But her imagination was abruptly ended, for the light came back.

With a resigned gesture, David Borha fell silent.

Lucy Idahaso looked at her children on the floor. She remembered her husband.

Then she assumed an attitude of mournful dignity, with downcast eyes, she said: "I think you should go now. I want to sleep. You should also stop coming in the night. The neighbours will talk when they see you."

"Very well," he said firmly, looking at the dirty floor. "I'll go."

David Borha walked out of the shack into the dark courtyard. The darkness which filled his eyes began to penetrate into his soul.

"What type of life am I leading?" he asked himself.

His loneliness, his conversation with Lucy Idahaso made him conscious of a great need for companionship and love.

He went into his car and drove away from the slum area to the wealthy part of the city.

He began to feel a sense of emptiness and a need to occupy himself with something. He was struck by the vanity of his purposelessness.

He thought of driving home, but remembered there would be no one waiting for him. He then decided to go to a restaurant.

44

After sipping his drink, an intolerable nervous depression assailed him. He left the restaurant and drove home.

At home he felt tired as a result of the sapping heat of Lagos and from the sense of emptiness that always remained with him when he abandoned himself to his fantasy.

After Lucy Idahaso had struggled and saved some money for her fare to Benin, she went to prison to get her husband's written permission to sell his land. She dressed in a colourful attire.

Her husband did not expect to see his wife when he was called to the prison's visitors' room. He was, therefore, extremely happy when he saw her.

She told him the purpose of her visit. He sought permission from the warders and wrote a letter, authorising her to sell his piece of land.

When the visit ended, Garuba Idahaso stood by watching his wife. The warder, in charge of the visitors' room, threw a glance of approval to him.

Garuba Idahaso watched his wife until she disappeared. He thought of his wife, children and his innocence. Faith, sincerity had betrayed him. A tragic sense no longer existed in him. Things began to appear to him as senseless.

On Wednesday morning, his wife took a bus to Benin. She sold the piece of land for six hundred pounds. On her way back to Lagos, the bus in which she was travelling suddenly came to a roadblock. She saw masked men shooting in the air, with automatic rifles. They surrounded the bus. Two of them climbed into the bus.

Lucy Idahaso gazed in a terrifying manner as the masked men searched the passengers.

45

"Oh life! Do you strike twice?" she asked herself silently, as one of the masked men came to her.

"It can strike ten times," the nose of the rifle seemed to say to her.

"Stand up!" ordered the masked man, pointing a rifle to her. She stood up shivering in fear.

He searched her and found six hundred pounds in notes tied in a rag.

"It's over," explained the masked man, after he grabbed the money.

The next moment she heard more gun shots as the robbers deflated the tyres of the bus.

Lucy Idahaso and the rest of the passengers descended from the bus, after the robbers had gone.

She stood together with the passengers under a sky covered with a huge black cloud. Like a gigantic pall, the cloud lay over the whole area, seeming to symbolise the extinction of her hope.

Then the rain came down. Lucy Idahaso with the passengers climbed into the bus.

An open lorry came after some hours. She and the rest of the passengers squeezed into it.

She arrived in Lagos very late, drenched and penniless.

That night she saw herself poor, lonely, with two children and David Borha playing the role of Don Juan.

When she woke up the following morning, the sun was shining and light was filtering into the untidy shack from every side. But the brightness of the day did not last long. After a moment the clouds covered the sun, and the rain started, turning the day into a grey one, symbolising the greyness of her life.

From that day, the life of Lucy Idahaso was one of

hard work. Apart from her normal petty trade of selling fruits, she sought all types of jobs in the houses of rich people. She washed for their wives. Ground pepper, tomatoes and onions for them. Cooked and pounded yams for herself. Her hands became rough and began to crack. Some wrinkles appeared on her face, and her eyes puffed out because of lack of sleep.

David Borha kept coming. He offered help and seduction, she turned both down.

After two years Lucy Idahaso's physical appearance changed. She looked as if she was over fifty.

A few months to the end of her husband's prison term, a new evidence surfaced. An article appeared in the *Sunday Herald* in which a well-known criminal, Moses Adi, confessed how he had dumped a briefcase he snatched on Garuba Idahaso. The police arrested Moses Adi, who confirmed his confessions in the newspaper to them. An investigation by the police also revealed what he said to be correct.

Garuba Idahaso was released and told that it was a tremendous miscarriage of justice. The day he came out of prison he could not recognise his wife for she had aged very much.

"Is this really you?" he said to her when she embraced him outside the prison yard.

"Yes," she replied. "Let's go home, I'll tell you all about it."

MOONSTRUCK

Saratu, a beautiful young woman, married to Umaru, a shopkeeper, had just finished cooking dinner for the family. She ran to the hill at the eastern corner of the house and watched the twilight giving way to the luminous glow of the moon. Brilliant flares of the amber red fire dimmed the luminous glow as the moon spurted up, lighting up the small town. Her recent discovery of watching the moon come up, when she found herself in a house on a hilly area, gave her great pleasure. Often when enjoying such a pleasure, she forgot to say her evening prayers, which were supposed to be said just after the sun set. She was coming down from the hill when she heard the voice of her mother-in-law, Jaku. She ran into her room, fetched a kettle and began to perform ablution for her prayers; for she knew her mother-in-law was only calling her to find out if she had said her prayers.

"You mean you have not said your prayers?" Jaku began. "What have you been doing? What type of a woman are you? Didn't they train you in your home to pray in time? Well, listen, in this house you must worship Allah. Don't let me see you repeat it again."

Saratu went on performing her ablution without saying a word. When she finished she went into her room, but Jaku followed her saying, "I am beginning to doubt you. Might be you really don't pray. You only perform ablution to deceive me."

Jaku sat down watching Saratu praying. She left the room after her daughter-in-law finished praying. Later when Saratu took dinner to her she refused it.

49

"What have you cooked?" Jaku wanted to know.

"It is only beans with groundnut oil," responded Saratu.

"Don't you know I am allergic to groundnut oil?"

"I don't know. Moreover there is no butter in the house."

"That does not mean there is none in town, with all the fulanis around."

"I am sorry, it will not happen again."

"Take your food. By the Prophet, I will not touch the food of a woman who does not pray in time."

Saratu returned to her room with the food, partly puzzled and partly irritated. She complained to Umaru, about his mother's tantrums.

"Take it easy, don't let it bother you," he cooled her down when he heard some traces of anger in her voice. "I am sure she will change when she gets familiar with you."

"How soon? I have been in this house for more than six months, but her actions seem to be getting worse. What shall I do now? I can't find butter in this night and I don't want to leave her without . . ." Saratu paused when she saw Jaku coming.

"Your wife wants to starve me," Jaku descended on her son from her height of motherhood. "Yes, she married you to kill me. What else, that's why she cooks what I can't eat. Are you going to leave your mother in the hands of your wicked wife? Merciful Allah! A son sits down and lets his wife starve his mother in the name of marriage. Are you going to do something before I invoke a curse on you?"

"I am sorry, mother, let me go and buy you some food in the town," Umaru said, standing up. "Calm yourself, I am sorry. Your daughter didn't know you

50

are allergic to groundnut oil. In the future she will always ask your preference in food."

"Who is my daughter?" Jaku asked in disgust. "Allah forbids! Not a woman who does not pray in time."

Umaru picked up a dish and went in search of food. When he returned, he apologised again and promised his mother, "It will never happen again."

"It is high time, if you don't intend to let your wife make you end in hell," Jaku pattered.

In the middle of the night, when the moon was high and the town basked in its light, Saratu felt the desire to ease herself. She got up and went to the latrine. She was about to go back to her room when the brilliance of the moonlight and the stillness of the night caught her attention. So she stood on the doorway of her room agape at the occurrence. A distant sound of drumming crept in the silence. She smiled to herself, for she recognised the drumming. It was coming from her hometown, not far away from where she was now married. The beatings of the drum invoked memories of her girlhood. She had danced many times to that particular tune. It was still the same drummers, playing at the same square, where she had danced when she was a girl. It was not only girls who danced in her town, married women danced too, unlike in the town where she was now living. Nobody regarded dancing as revolting, their town was more tolerant. People did what they liked as long as they did not reach the extreme. True, people were religious, but they hesitated to criticise you for praying late, for they regarded others as mature.

Her recollections were brought to an end by the

51

song of the wind when the music abruptly stopped. She was started until she realised what it was when the music resumed. This time it came louder, accompanied by the song of the girls. Suddenly, Saratu found herself joining the chorus and dancing to the distant music. She danced on and on until she was covered by her sweat.

When the drums and the girls stopped, she heard footsteps. Her heart thumped, and she looked towards the courtyard and saw a woman standing. She quickly ran to her room and shut the door, for she knew it was her mother-in-law.

The following morning, Saratu went, as usual, to salute her diminutive mother-in-law of over sixty. Jaku uttered no word after repeated greetings from Saratu. She only gazed at her, muttering as if she were intoning a prayer. Saratu rose from her knees and was about to go out of the room when suddenly Jaku spoke in a malevolent voice.

"May Allah make fence between you and me."

Saratu looked at Jaku wondering what offence she had committed to deserve such a wrath early in the morning.

"Don't ever come to greet me in the morning after you have contaminated yourself with bad jinns. Only jinns stand on the doorway in the middle of the night, not to talk of dancing and singing to music from only Allah knows where," Jaku addressed Saratu.

"I was only enjoying the moonlight," Saratu said.

"Are you a jinn? Only jinns derive pleasure at such hours. The moonlight is made for them while the sunlight for us, humans. I came out yesterday because I was hard pressed. But every step I made I

52

intoned a powerful prayer to counteract any danger of the hidden ones and the owners of the night. By Allah, the way I saw you — bare breast, bare head and dancing to that music.

Oh no! you must be very careful. You don't play with the owners of the night. They will destroy you promptly. And through you destroy everyone in this house. Don't you know that music was typical of the jinns? Who else could be drumming and singing at that hour! If you don't know, jinns normally perform their marriage ceremony when the moon is waxing. From its tune it surely was the music of the marriage ceremony of the daughters of the king of jinns. And you joined them in dancing and singing. They will surely think you are mocking them. Who knows whether you have stepped on their younger ones and have broken their tender limbs. They were all over the place yesterday. You are destroying yourself. Mark my words jinns avenge at the promptest."

Saratu walked out of Jaku's room without saying anything to her chiding though she was disturbed by it. After both her husband and mother-in-law had gone out of the house, she decided to visit her girlhood friend, Nana, who was married to a tailor, for a change: She walked the little distance dreading she would meet someone who would recognise her and tell her husband. She did not seek any permission from him to visit her friend because she knew he would not allow her for fear of his mother's disapproval.

"What, you in broad daylight! I can't believe it, hope nothing is wrong," Nana said when she saw Saratu.

"For once I decided to take a risk," Saratu began even before she sat down. "I am feeling as if I am in a prison. I am fed up with that bitch. She is full of superstitions and religion. A real fanatic. And she wants to impose her belief on me. There is nothing I do that is correct. Everything I do I have to seek her permission. I am married to two husbands."

"Don't let her worry you. Mothers-in-law are always like that. You have to stand up to her tantrum."

"She is the worst I have ever seen."

"Okay, tell your husband to do something. He loves you very much. I heard him telling my husband. He made me jealous of you. I believe my husband never talks about me like that. I am sure if you talk to him he will do something."

"He is a mummy's boy, completely under her yoke. I have talked to him several times, but he did nothing. If that bitch were a man no woman would have married him. What a tyrant! And always talking of Allah as if she were the Prophet."

"Then advise your husband to get her another place."

"He cannot face her with that. She rules him. She is ruthless also. If I give her a chance she can thrash me. The other day I was grinding corn and singing when she came out with a cornstalk ordering me to be quiet or else she would flog me."

"Oh, no!" exclaimed Nana.

"Really, she considers singing as sinful as drinking alcohol. She says only Satan's followers sing."

"What will happen if she finds you have come here today?"

"I will just pack my few things and head for my

54

father's house. For I know she will order her son to divorce me. She does not allow me to raise my voice so that passers-by may not hear it. A married woman's voice, she says, is only meant for her husband and no other man. And you know how I like to sing and dance. She caught me dancing and singing yesterday night and ..."

"Did you scare the hell out of the bitch?"

"Not at all. She stood by watching, but early in the morning she dressed me down. Only jinns do that, so she chided me."

They laughed. On her way out she met Nana's brother, Hamza, a tall, slender man with a wide mouth.

"Saratu!" Hamza exclaimed.

"Hamza!" she called out. He had now become a man of the world, she thought. He had wanted to marry her but his parents had disagreed.

"Hope I will see more of you. I will be staying for a month or two," Hamza said.

Saratu went home thinking of Hamza, but to prove to herself that she was still a good wife she began to prepare a delicious dinner for her husband.

In the evening when both her husband and his mother returned, Saratu found herself unable to say a word to either of them.

"Your behaviour is sacrilegious," her mother-in-law scolded her. "He is your husband and I am his mother. Yet you cannot utter a word of welcome to us. Only those in Satan's circle refuse to greet people they come across, not to talk of the people you live with. Don't you know that you can only go to heaven through him and me."

"I don't want your heaven!"

"Blasphemer! The Prophet, be my witness," Jaku exclaimed. Turning to her son she continued, "On the Koran, I told you before, the woman is an unbeliever, and she intends to turn this house into the hottest part of the hell."

"By Allah, she is a true muslim, mother!" Umaru exclaimed.

"No true muslim utters what she says."

"She will stop."

"It is too late. Satan has won her over."

In the night Saratu told her husband of her inability to become the model his mother wished her to be. She appealed to him to find ways of diffusing the situation before it exploded.

"I love you, but I cannot go against the wish of my mother. I know she is difficult and rigid in her religious outlook," her husband said to her.

"Then you choose between me and her."

"You are asking me to choose between my trousers and my gown."

"You do something to save our marriage. I love you, but she is making my life miserable."

"I know and I sympathise with you. Be a little patient. People will condemn me for not obeying her. I must do as she wishes."

In the next few days, Saratu saw Hamza several times. Their meetings revived their former feelings for one another. And the more they thought of the barrier which separated them to live as lovers, the stronger was the impulse that urged them towards one another, until Saratu yielded to his love. However, though she yielded to his love, she turned down his request to abandon her husband and follow him when he was leaving the town. She continued to live with her husband as if nothing had happened, especially since neither he nor his mother knew about her secret meetings with Hamza.

One day Jaku found Saratu in the entrance hall of the house peeping at passers-by. Jaku was shocked to the extent she could not say a word to her daughter-in-law for finding her breaking one of the cardinals of purdah. Saratu made no attempt to run inside the house, as women in purdah normally did when caught in such acts. She stood looking at the people without paying any attention to Jaku.

"Bloody prostitute!" Jaku screamed, slamming the door of the house.

Saratu only kept looking at her without attempting to go in the house.

"Get in, if you still regard yourself as a married woman," shouted Jaku. "I am sure you were a prostitute before you hooked my son. I can see it from your eyes. Are you waiting for a man? Who is he? No wonder you were coming out in the middle of the night. You were meeting men. You wait until we are asleep then you sneak and open doors for them. How many do you have in a night? Swear on the Koran if you have not been doing that. By Allah, you have ruined this house."

"Don't touch me," Saratu warned her mother-in-law when she attempted to drag her inside the house.

"Will you kill me if I touch you? You look a murderer. How many people have you murdered before you came here? I know you don't love my son, you want to kill him. You bitch!" Jaku kicked with her leg in the event of which she fell down. The contents of the bundle she was carrying scattered all over the hall.

"You have kicked me and broken my legs. Merciful Allah! Save me from a murderer," Jaku screamed. From where she lay she got a missile and threw it at Saratu, but it missed her. Saratu walked away to her room without caring to help her mother-in-law.

But no sooner had she sat down when Jaku entered the room screaming. "Kill me if it will make it easier for you to have love affairs. By Allah, you have been bringing men in your matrimonial room."

"I don't need to bring men in this home," Saratu exploded in anger. "If you want to know I had an affair with a man in a room akin to those in Arabian Nights. You can tell your baby to divorce me. And get out of my room before I break your head."

"You will surely go," Jaku said, walking out of the room. "My son has no choice. You married him in order to bring him someone else's child. Well, retribution has caught up with you. Today is the end of your adulterous life in this house. And may Allah protect us from your sinful acts."

Jaku went and sat in the entrance hall of the house waiting for her son. As soon as she saw him coming she began to sob.

"What is the problem, mother?"

"Your wife," she said in sobs.

"What has happened to her?"

"Sit down and write a letter divorcing her," Jaku commanded as her sobs came to an end.

"What has she done, mother?"

"She is no longer marriage worthy. She has

58

confessed to me, after she kicked me down, that she had an affair with a man. I am not surprised. I advised you not to marry her.

"Well, this is it, you have all along been living with an adulterous wife. If she is pregnant don't accept it, it can't be your child. Only Allah knows how many men she slept with since she came to this house." Jaku explained to Umaru.

"All right, mother, I will go and speak to her," Umaru replied.

"To speak to her! It seems you don't believe me."

"I believe you, mother."

"Then there is no need for you to speak to her. Write a letter divorcing her three times and make sure she does not sleep in this house."

"I have to get someone to write the letter, mother. Let me go inside and pick up something."

"You are not picking up anything. The bitch will tell you I am lying. She may even attempt to kill you. Her plan is to see me and you dead. So that she can inherit the house and turn it into a brothel."

"She cannot kill me, mother. I am stronger than her, though she is taller. I want to ask her why she kicked you down. Whatever you did to her she has no right to kick you."

"Just go and get someone to write you that letter. There is nothing which that woman cannot do."

"For Allah's sake, let me go in. I promise to do exactly what you wish."

"All right, since you say Allah, you can go, but don't stay long."

When Umaru entered Saratu's room he found her packing her few belongings.

"What are you doing?" he asked her.

59

"Didn't she tell you?"

"Even if she told me that does not mean you pack without my permission. You are my wife. Didn't you say you love me? Tell me what has happened?"

"You will never have the courage to go against her wish. So what is the point of my telling you my side of the story. I have heard what she told you. Is the letter ready? Am I to receive it from her?"

"I am not divorcing you. I love you and I won't let you go."

"It is true that I had an affair with a man. I was not lying."

Umaru felt the stab of pain in his stomach. He sat down. "No, no, you are lying," he said, standing up. "You only said it to annoy her. She makes your life miserable, so you decided to pay her back by hitting her where she feels most, because you know she is pious . . ."

"Pious or a fanatic!" exclaimed Saratu.

"Okay, whatever you say. I know you are not as irreligious as my mother thinks you are. But you want her to believe that you don't give a damn about religion. You rebelled against her because she tormented you. I know you very well to detect your lies. You will never yield to anybody's love. It is me you love and no one else. So I cannot see you committing such an act. You never had an affair with any man. You are innocent, but you want to show my mother that you are worldly-wise. No Saratu, you are too pure to think in that direction. It's your imagination. Stop deluding yourself. Come back to reality. Stop dreaming."

"I am not dreaming, Umaru. I am facing reality. I have been living in a house where every one refuses to face the facts of life. Well, I have grown up, I am no longer a child. I am fed up with the whole thing. Go and bring me my letter. It is a fact I had an affair with a man. You know him . . . . Hamza. I wanted to marry him but fate didn't allow it. And now you have heard, so run and have my letter written. Give it to her to bring to me. That's what she wants. I am not sleeping in this house. I will go, even without your letter."

"You are not going," he said, holding her bundle.

"Oh, I am going. It won't work any more. Let us face it, I am no longer the virtuous wife. If it is the bundle you want, you can have it," she pushed the bundle to him and bolted away. He dropped the bundle, grabbed her knees sobbing and pleading, "Please don't go, don't abandon me. Don't leave me, I love you."

Saratu pulled herself away and ran out of the house.

A HOUSE IN THE DARK

"Maybe I'm going to my death," Fatima said aloud. She contemplated a little, fidgeted with her wrapper and added, "It's better than to live with that old dirty man as my husband."

She walked towards the flickering light, wondering what it might be. She remembered people said hyena's eyes could look like that in the moonless and starless night. Covering her eyes with a part of her wrapper, she walked on, as the wind started to blow the semi-desert sand about.

"It's all the fault of my father, he is to blame for all that has happened to me," she said with a frown as she stumbled on a ridge in a farm, after she left the main track.

"What would mother have thought if she were alive when my father gave me out as a gift to Maigoro, of all the people who wanted to marry me. Agreed I am not the prettiest girl in town, but that does not mean father should give me out as a wife, like a goat, to a man more than 30 years older than myself," she mused.

She recalled how she cried on the day she was told she was given to Maigoro. She threatened to throw herself into a well, but her father did not change his mind.

"If all goes well and I am alive by tomorrow I will be in the city, where neither Maigoro nor my father can find me. I will then give my body to whomever I like. It's bye for marriage, I will be and remain a prostitute for the rest of my life," she said, loudly. She bumped on a shrub and fell down. She got up and cursed Maigoro. He too had something to do with this.

She then recollected the day she was taken to his house, six months ago. He came to her, smelling donkey shit.

She sprang up from the bed. "I will not sleep in the same hut with you," she said, running out of the hut. On that night she went and slept in the hut of his senior wife, Bilki.

From then onward she continued to run and sleep in Bilki's hut whenever Maigoro entered her hut in the night.

"That Bilki, she treated me like her daughter," Fatima said to herself. "Well, I am more or less like her daughter, with Jumai, who is older than me, as her third child."

"Hm, how could a father do that. Me, a girl of 18, marrying a man over 55. Well, I will never go back to him," she resolved to herself.

The barking of dogs shattered her thoughts. She was relieved. "It's a house after all" she said aloud as she saw three thatches against the sky when the lightning flashed.

After looking at the dark threatening sky, she saw a hurricane lamp. She walked towards it, and heard the dogs coming to her.

"All right, Shago and Fari," a voice shouted to the dogs that stopped barking.

"Who's there in a night like this?" a man's voice inquired.

"It's a stranger on her way to the city looking for a place to hide from the impending storm," Fatima responded, in a thrill voice.

"Who will not welcome a stranger in such a night.

Come, you are welcome," the man said, coming towards her.

She walked and reached him.

"I know you will come. Praise be to Allah. My grand-daughter has come back. Ever since you left us, Rakiya, I have been praying to Allah that you may return. Now my prayer has been heard," the old man said, raising the hurricane lamp to her face and looking at her.

"Oh my God! What's happening again. Am I bumping on a lunatic? Allah have mercy on me, help me," she said in her mind.

"Your room is still as you left it," the old man continued. "Sometimes I go into it and cry. Kasimu, I will say to myself, go and pray, Allah will hear you. Well here you are, wait I will bring matches before the rain comes."

He came out of his hut and she followed the stooped figure into a hut in the centre of the house. He stroked the matches, lit a hurricane lamp.

"Thanks be to Allah," he said again, looking at her face.

Fatima looked at him, musing, "He does not look that lunatic. Maybe his eyes are bad."

"Do you want something to eat, Rakiya?" he asked her.

"Fatima," she wanted to correct him. "No, no thanks, I am not hungry, I want to sleep," she replied.

"You will never change. I was afraid that you would change. How long was it since you left us ... Oh let me see...yes, six months ..... Oh let me not disturb you ... you must be tired," he said, going out of the room.

65

"Tanimu, Tanimu, Rakiya has come back. Yes, your sister has returned," she heard him saying into the other hut.

She looked around the hut, saw some woman's dresses. After blowing off the light, she lay on the cornstalk bed, praying tomorrow would come soon, and Kasimu, the old man, would recognise that she was not his grand-daughter.

Then she heard thunder and saw her room filled with light. And the rain began to pour heavily.

In the morning when Fatima woke up she went to the hut of Kasimu, hoping that he would now recognise that she was not his grand-daughter. When entering the hut she saw a heap of earth behind it, which she believed to be a grave.

"Thank you very much for the bed. Now I must continue with my journey," she was about to say when a boy of fifteen dressed only in shorts came in.

"Tanimu, look at your sister, she did not change," Kasimu said, pointing to Fatima with his hand, which was holding a rosary.

Tanimu looked at Fatima, then at his grandfather who was now stroking his grey beard with his left hand. A kind, rather pathetic smile appeared on his handsome face.

"Welcome Rakiya. It's nice you have come back," he said to Fatima.

"Oh merciful Allah, what is all this. Can't they see I am not Rakiya?" she said silently.

"I am going to untether the goats. They seem eager to put to pasture," Tanimu said, going out of the hut.

"Do that Tanimu," Kasimu said. Turning to

66

Fatima he went on, "Rakiya, when you went away, Halima, a woman from Nasari compound was helping us with food. Two days ago, she told me she would be travelling to the city for her daughter's marriage. We have just finished the food yesterday. There is only a little porridge left. So you better make some today," Kasimu said, scratching his long back with his left hand.

"Look at this old man. I must tell him I am not Rakiya. I am Fatima," she mused. But she remembered that even if she left the house she would be going to the city. And making food is one of the first odd jobs a debutant undergoes in prostitution. "After all, I am to stay with the experienced ones to learn the art," she mused.

"The millet for making the porridge is still in your hut," Kasimu said, breaking the chain of her thoughts.

She went into her hut and found the millet. She got a mortar under a tree and began to pound the millet. Kasimu came out, sat down and began to twine ropes.

Late in the afternoon, Tanimu returned from the pasture. He undressed in the courtyard of the house and began to wash himself, without saying a word to any of them.

Fatima ran a glance over his fresh body, musing. "He washes himself better than my stinking husband who never washes."

One morning, Tanimu went to his grandfather.

"Grandpa," he said, "You don't want me to go to pasture with Rakiya?"

"Why not, you can go with her, go ask her," Kasimu said, without looking at his grandson.

"Rakiya, Grandpa says we can go to pasture together," Tanimu said to Fatima.

"Pasture! Do these lunatics think they have a slave. I better go and tell that old scraggy man that I am not his grand-daughter. He is going too far," she thought.

"Yes, have you forgotten. You know we used to play and eat wild fruits," Tanimu said, shattering her thoughts.

She looked at his handsome face and saw him gazing at her. "Hm, better to go to pasture with this handsome boy than staying with that old man," she decided in her mind.

"We shall go to pasture together, Tanimu. Let me put on my sandals," she said, going into her hut, with a strange new expression on her face.

When she came out, she found him waiting with a stick, a knife and a gourd slang on his shoulder.

"Your delicious porridge," he said, smiling when he saw her look at the ground.

Though Fatima had never been to pasture in her life, she found no difficulty in following Tanimu, for he did most of the running and shouting in efforts to control the goats.

At noon when the sun reached the centre of the sky, and it was too hot for even the goats, she and Tanimu found a big tree and sat under it.

Tanimu ran to a nearby farm, dug out sweet potatoes and came back.

"We will roast it here," he said, digging the ground with his knife.

He then buried the sweet potatoes and made a fire on top of it, as she watched in amusement. "Very practical," she said, silently.

"Let me get us some fruits," he said, climbing the tree.

After he picked and dropped down some fruits, he began to climb down when a branch of a tree held his shorts.

"Help me, cut it with the knife," Tanimu said to Fatima.

She reached the branch from the ground and cut it clumsily. Tanimu fell down.

"Are you hurt?" she asked softly, bending down over him.

He said nothing but lay down closing his eyes.

Fear gripped her.

"Help me Allah! Tanimu, are you hurt?" she asked, sitting down. She put his head on her lap and began to touch his face gently with her hand.

He opened his eyes. Then closed them and opened them, smiling.

"You aren't hurt. You just want to rest on my lap," she uttered, feeling relieved.

"Yes, don't stop touching my face," he pleaded, touching hers.

She smiled while he moved his hand to the curve of her breast.

"Oh no, don't do that," she wished to say, but the sight of his handsome face silenced her.

"Do you like it?" he asked, reaching the nipple of her breast.

She quivered and he felt it.

The following night when she blew off the light and lay on the bed, she heard steps coming to her hut.

"Rakiya, are you awake?" Tanimu asked gently, on her door.

"Is that Tanimu? I am awake," Fatima responded, getting up from the bed.

"Yes, it's me, may I come in?" he said, his voice trembling.

"Why not?" she put in, opening the door for him. He came in as she struck a match and lit the lamp.

"I can't sleep," he said softly.

"Me too, Tanimu," she replied, looking at him, sitting down on the floor.

"No, come here on the bed. There are ants on the floor," she retorted, as the upper part of her wrapper which had ridden up to cover her breasts, slipped down, revealing her firm breasts.

"Has Kasimu slept?" she inquired, after he sat down.

"Yes, that's why I came in," he responded, looking at her breasts.

She tried to cover her breasts with her wrapper as she became aware of his gaze. But Tanimu held her hands saying, "Please don't, they are beautiful."

She smiled, remembering that nobody ever expressed an appreciation on any part of her body. Then they heard the crying of hyenas, which silenced the distant barking of the dogs.

"Are you afraid?" she asked him, toying with the end of her wrapper.

"No, but once hyenas came here and killed some goats," he replied.

Then they gazed at each other. He buried his head on her lap.

In the morning when Tanimu was going out of her hut, his grandfather, Kasimu, saw him. Kasimu threw a glance at his grandson, signifying his disapproval of what he had seen.

70

Tanimu understood the meaning of the glance but he continued to sleep in Fatima's hut. He went further by going into her hut at any time of the day he liked.

His grandfather saw this but did nothing.

One morning, after Tanimu had left her hut, Fatima lay awake and pondered. She realised she had not known many men. But of the few she had known, none had truly possessed her like Tanimu. He had entered into those dim recesses of her spirit which she kept inviolate for herself and for the man who mattered.

That meant Tanimu mattered, she said to herself. She, however, felt that there was something in the house which she could not understand. What would become of her relation with Tanimu when she understood those things? She remembered how she set her foot into that house, she realised she was coming to hide from an impending storm. But now she was finding herself in another storm. Would she be able to find a place to hide from it?

One Friday afternoon, Fatima saw a woman of about 45, of medium height, coming to the house. She concluded in her mind that she was Halima, the woman who was helping Tanimu and his grandfather with food.

When she was alone with Halima, Fatima told her what had happened to her since her arrival in that house.

"I am forgetting I am Fatima. They all call me Rakiya, but there is an air of mystery in the house. I can't see how they could mistake me for their Rakiya," she said, gloomily to Halima.

"What's in a name? Don't bother yourself. After

71

all, if I get you right you and Tanimu seem to be in love, the best thing then for you is to stay. You never know what you will encounter in the city," Halima responded.

Fatima felt glad at hearing the thought that filled her mind put in words.

"But it sometimes torments me when I think Tanimu loves me because he thinks I am his sister," Fatima said, looking at Halima pathetically.

"Don't think, live from day to day. That's what we do when we find ourselves in a situation we cannot control," Halima advised her with an air of resignation to fate.

After Halima had gone, Fatima pondered whether Rakiya was just a figment of Kasimu's and his grandson's imagination. There was something missing, but she could not put her finger on it. She resolved in her mind that she would find whether Rakiya had really existed.

One night when Tanimu had come to her hut, she held his hand and said, "Tanimu, darling, can you do me a favour?"

"I will be glad to do it. You know I love you," he replied, looking at her.

She pressed his hand. "Are you sure I am Rakiya, your sister?"

Tanimu said nothing but gazed at her, then at her breasts.

"I am asking you a favour. You said you will do it for me," she said, caressing his chin.

"It's Halima who told you," he responded, not looking at her.

"No, she told me nothing," she said, working her hand on him.

72

"I know you are not Rakiya, my sister," he replied, looking down.

"Why do you then call me Rakiya?" she inquired again.

Tanimu fell silent.

"Why did Rakiya leave you? Come, tell me Tanimu, my darling," she said, putting her hand around him.

"She just ran away. One morning we woke up and found she was not at home," he replied.

"Did you love her the way you love me?" she asked.

"Why, are you jealous?" he responded.

"No, I just want to know," she pleaded, putting his head on her lap.

"I will tell you if you want to know," he began, stroking her wrapper. "One day we were sitting down under that big tree, where you and I sat down the other day, when we started to argue. A wrestling ensued. Though she was older than myself, I managed to be on top of her. Then my hand touched her breasts accidently. I felt a quiver, then I touched it again and again. At first she frowned at it, but later she too liked it. From then we began to sleep together as you and I do now," he said, as he stretched his hand to touch her breast.

"No, it's not your sister's breast. It's not Rakiya's breast," she said to him.

Tanimu sat up and left the hut immediately.

Fatima lay awake. She remembered that at first she had felt Tanimu's daring acts of coming to her hut and possessing her body at any time he liked, had been a bit too much. But now when he left her alone in the hut, she realised how his absence

73

overcame her, and that she had been deceiving herself that his demand and possessing of her body, at any time he liked, was the sole reason of her staying in that house.

The following morning, Tanimu did not go to pasture with her.

"What's the matter, Rakiya? Please don't go away. Promise you will stay," Kasimu said, when he saw how gloomy she looked that morning.

"You will never see your Rakiya again. No girl who has conscience can stay when she made it with her younger brother. And you better get it in your head that I am not Rakiya," she wanted to scream out at him. But then she realised that she had left her husband and was now giving her body to a boy of sixteen "I promise, I will not go away," she said, looking at him.

"Did you fight again with your brother?" Kasimu asked her.

"Fight again," Fatima said, silently. "So the old man knew what had happened between his grandchildren."

When Tanimu returned from pasture, he said nothing to her.

She looked at him, "Go away. Get out of my sight. You are disgusting. No heart, no honour. You lie, you never loved me. I am just a figment of your sister . . . and how I love you," she wanted to tell him.

For a week Tanimu did not talk or enter her hut. Every night Fatima lay expecting every moment that he would come. She both feared and wanted his coming. But he did not come.

On the eighth night she went to his hut.

74

"Is it Rakiya?" Tanimu asked, when he heard her hitting at his door.

"Open! Open! It's not Rakiya, you know who it is," she replied.

He opened the door and let her in.

"Why did you come?" he asked, lighting the lamp.

"Because I love you, Tanimu," she replied, looking at his fresh adolescent body. "Is he capable of loving any one after he made it with his sister?" she wondered in her mind.

"I don't love you. I love Rakiya and it's her alone I love. She was the only person I am capable of loving," he said, looking at her, and the hatred she saw in his face frightened and bewildered her.

"Don't you know you are my life? Are you not ashamed to love your sister?" she asked him.

"No, what have I done to be ashamed of? One must have someone to hang on," he said, coldly.

"And you can only hang on her. Why not hang on me?" she pleaded, looking at him.

"You know, she was the only one I love. Oh my Rakiya," he said, sobbing. "Oh how I love her."

"Tell me what really happened to her?" she inquired, holding him.

"I will tell you," he said, controlling his sobs. "Rakiya wanted to go away after we had been making love for some days. She said she could not bear it ... I told her I could not survive without her. One Friday night I saw her coming out of the hut with a bundle of her clothes. I held her, we struggled and she hit me several times. I had my knife with me. I did not know when ..."

And sobs cut short his words.

"Then what?" Fatima shouted, shaking him.

75

"Then she fell dead," he uttered hopelessly, looking at her, hoping to see some expression of sympathy from her, but Fatima showed none.

"What did you do, did your grandfather tell the authorities?" she inquired, her face bore a stern expression.

"No, he helped me bury her behind his hut," he said.

"Did he know you made it with her?" she asked, still shaking him.

"Yes, he knew, but what could he do? He too made it with his younger sister. That was why he left the city, came here and settled down," Tanimu said.

Fatima took off her hands from him when she became conscious she was holding him. She looked at her hands which held him and felt an immense repulsion. She remembered the flickering light which drove her to the house in that dark night. That light was only a glimpse into what symbolised that house — a terrible glow of fire in the dark night.

She turned to go out of the room when she came face to face with Kasimu. He held her with his bony hands. She looked at him in askance.

"It's true what Tanimu told you. I have heard it, your shouts woke me up. Please, you promised not to go away, stay with us. What is your name?"

"You revolting, scoundrel old dirty man. You will never know my name," she wanted to scream on his face, but she restrained herself.

"Rakiya — that's my name," she said, freeing herself from his grip and running out into the moonlit night.

CONFESSIONS OF AN ARMED ROBBER

Obi Chukwu, a short, stout man of 29 with some traces of beard and whiskers on his face, gave a brief interview on the platform of the execution, saying to himself: "There's a shock for the country — A Mysterious Armed Robber Executed."

The sound of the six madison automatic rifles shattered his thoughts. He became aware that he was watching a public execution of the armed robbers at Bar Beach in Lagos.

He looked at the head of a dying man, lolling about and muttering some words. Then he heard a single shot which silenced the man. He stared at the soldier who fired the shot. With curiosity, he watched as the doctor examined the bodies and declared them dead. Edging his way through the crowd he saw the labourers putting the bodies in the wooden coffins.

He saw the soldier who fired the last shot and said "Do you think the last shot was necessary?"

"Who are you?" the soldier asked, staring at him.

"I'm somebody," Obi Chukwu retorted.

"You are crazy," the soldier said, walking away.

Obi Chukwu walked to another soldier.

"Why do you always execute them in a group?" he asked.

"Go ask government," replied the soldier.

He moved through the crowd to the funeral van.

"Where are you going to bury them?" Obi Chukwu asked the labourers, who were putting the coffins into the van.

"What's your business?" the labourers inquired.

"None, just want to know."

"You want to know so that you can go and take their hearts to make juju. We will pour acid which will turn their bodies into dust," one of the labourers replied.

"Please do that so that their spirits can never rise," a tall man with a wide mouth spoke from the crowd.

Obi Chukwu looked at the man and said, "They can't execute their spirits."

"Why? Because they were your brothers?" the man inquired.

"All men are brothers," said Obi Chukwu.

"Not armed robbers. They might be yours, though."

"Yes, they were my brothers," responded Obi Chukwu.

"You must be one of them," said the man.

"So what?" Obi Chukwu asked.

"Are you crazy? Maybe you have nothing to do," the man replied, walking away.

Obi Chukwu went and climbed the execution platform. After surveying the blood-stained posts against which the armed robbers were tied, he touched the ropes.

"Come down!" shouted a policeman.

"I'm just examining it," Obi Chukwu said to the policeman.

"Examining it or you want to make juju. Get out of there," the policeman replied, walking towards him.

Obi Chukwu came down.

"Tell me, did you ever arrest an armed robber?" Obi Chukwu asked the policeman.

"No, why?" inquired the policeman, looking at Obi Chukwu.

78

"Just curiosity," he replied, walking away.

The crowd drifted and Obi Chukwu walked to the police station. He roamed aimlessly within the vicinity of the station.

After some minutes, he saw a policeman coming towards him. He stood still in front of him.

"Have you ever arrested an armed robber?" Obi Chukwu asked the policeman.

"You got one for us?" the policeman asked.

"Yes, I'm an armed robber."

"You are crazy. You want to be locked up to eat government food," the policeman said, walking away.

After some hours, Obi Chukwu went and visited his friend who was a messenger in a government office.

"Ali, can I use your telephone?" he asked his friend when he saw there was no officer in the office.

"Yes, but be quick. I go toilet," Ali responded, going out of the office.

"Hello. . . . is that police. I know an armed robber at large," Obi Chukwu said, putting down the receiver.

Late in the afternoon, Obi Chukwu took a bus to his house. He found Ojo Taiwo, a man of medium height with tribal marks, and his fat, short wife, who were also tenants in the house, playing ayo on a mat in front of their room.

"Obi, have you been to the execution ground?" Ojo Taiwo asked after Obi Chukwu sat down.

"Yes, you know I always make it a point to go and watch how they die. Amadu was a coward. He did not take many bullets. He died easily like all lesser men," Obi Chukwu replied, looking at Ojo Taiwo.

"You have started your talk. One bullet can kill anybody. Also I heard Amadu did not die until they fired many bullets into him," responded Ojo Taiwo.

"Come off it. The soldier just wanted to waste government bullets. Amadu died before they even fired. He was no superman," said Obi Chukwu.

"Even a superman will die, Obi. You tie a man, you don't blindfold him, you arrange everything for his death, and even people are celebrating for it," Mrs. Taiwo said in a quiet, soft voice.

"Hm! leave them. The day I stand on that platform, I'll teach them a lesson. I'll show them I am a superman," Obi Chukwu exclaimed.

Ojo Taiwo looked at Obi Chukwu, saying, "What are you talking about? Do you want to be an armed robber? You talk too big or you are getting crazy."

"I'm not talking big. I'll teach the firing squad a lesson. I'll deliver a speech that will shake up this country."

"If you think you can do that, go, try to rob with a pair of scissors, that too is armed robbery," Ojo Taiwo retorted.

"A pair of scissors, me!" Obi Chukwu said, standing up and beating his chest. "I'm more than that. If you don't know I've killed with my bare hands and a dagger."

"Ah ha, things are happening. You took too much palm-wine today," Mrs. Taiwo concluded, looking at Obi Chukwu. "Let me advise you, don't talk whenever you're drunk."

80

"I'm as sober as a teetotaller can be," Obi Chukwu responded.

"Sit down, it's not a fight," Ojo Taiwo said. "What she means is that you can talk yourself to death. If policemen hear you, they will arrest you."

"Which policemen? They are not clever. If they had been smart, I would not have been here. They would have had me long time ago," Obi Chukwu boasted.

"I don't believe you. You can't rob anyone with violence. You just drank too much palm-wine," Ojo Taiwo insisted.

"Me!" exclaimed Obi Chukwu, brandishing his right hand. "I told you I've killed. I was ordered to do that by God. Go tell policemen."

"We won't tell policemen," Mrs. Taiwo said, addressing Obi Chukwu exclusively. "Retribution is like your dog, it follows you wherever you go."

"Leave him, he's drunk too much today. You better go and sleep, Obi. In the morning you will come back to your senses," Ojo Taiwo advised him.

Obi Chukwu went into his shack and thought of execution. He recalled the prostitute he had robbed and murdered. She was a plain looking woman in her late twenties, he had been watching her for days, at night in a corner, where she was soliciting for men. The urge to murder her came to him like a sexual urge. He took a dagger he had bought from a beggar and walked to the corner. They struck a bargain, and she agreed to take him to her room. They were walking in the deserted alley when he drew out his dagger and demanded all the money she had. She gave him in terror, begging him to leave her alone. He agreed to do that on condition she would make

81

love with him. When they reached her room, they both undressed, but instead of jumping to bed with her he strangled her. After that he stabbed her several times with the dagger. He left the sleepy house without meeting anyone, when he was sure she was dead.

When he woke up in the morning, he went to the armed robbery tribunal where he listened to the trial of some armed robbers. From there he proceeded to the police station where he roamed about.

One night, he was sitting down in his shack reading when he heard a knock on his door.

"Who's there," he asked, moving towards the door.

"It's Salami," his landlord replied.

He opened the door, Salami, a bulky man of forty-six in wrapper, walked in.

"You are always reading, Obi," Salami said, surveying the newspaper cuttings on public execution pasted on the four walls of the shack.

"Yes, I'm reading about Mighty Sam," Obi Chukwu replied, giving Salami the only chair in the room.

"Who's Mighty Sam?" asked Salami, with curiosity.

"He was an armed robber who refused to die after they shot many bullets into him, though he wasn't a superman. He put a good legal fight. There is his picture," Obi Chukwu explained, pointing to a picture on the wall.

"Hm! he refused to die," Salami exclaimed, looking at the picture.

"Yes he was brave, but the day I stand on that platform, even Mighty Sam will be forgotten."

Salami looked at Obi Chukwu and said, "I don't know why you're always preoccupied with armed robbery. Ojo and his wife were complaining to me that you talk too much and they think you'll get yourself into unnecessary trouble."

"Salami," Obi Chukwu said, sitting down on his bed. "Let me tell you one thing. It is not mere talk. I really robbed and killed a prostitute."

"Why a prostitute? You like them very much," Salami retorted.

"It's true I like them. But I robbed and murdered this one to punish society," explained Obi Chukwu.

"What, are you getting crazy? Has society done anything bad to you?"

"Society produces prostitutes and many other bad things. That's why I've turned into a desperate enemy of society, perhaps my hatred will only end with my life."

"Obi Chukwu, go back to your village. You need a native doctor. Please hear me, go back to your village," Salami urged him.

"There you are, one of them. I am no longer a member of the society. I reject its membership. My feeling for it is that of contempt and outrageousness for its values. In my eyes society is guilty and I have to punish it. You may not know that I am striving to be a god. I know people like you can't understand me. So good night," he said, standing up, showing the door to his landlord.

The following day, Salami went to the police and reported what Obi Chukwu told him. A search in his room revealed the dagger that he had used and press cuttings about the murder of the prostitute.

The police came and whisked him away. At the

83

trial, Obi Chukwu refused to have any legal advice. He was also found to be sane, and the judge was amazed with his high degree of intelligence. He was convicted to die by firing squad.

While Obi Chukwu was waiting for the governor's approval for his execution in the death cell he received no visitors. He knew he had no relatives who cared whether he lived or died. He watched with indifference when other condemned men had visitors.

Obi Chukwu listened to the conversations of other condemned men, hoping for the governor's clemency or a miracle to save their lives. He cared little for their talks and shared none of their hopes.

After a few weeks, he lost interest in other condemned men and only worried about himself. He gradually became aware that he was actually on his way to death but never dreaded it even for a while. The Chief Warder came and talked to him many times, but Obi Chukwu refused to reveal why he made no attempt to fight for his life.

"I came here to die," he said to the Chief Warder. "I would like your kindness if you can do nothing to help me get the governor's clemency."

"I don't understand, Obi Chukwu," the Chief Warder responded. "You are the first person to come here who does not want to live."

"I know you can't understand," Obi Chukwu said. "You're a lesser man."

He took the news of the governor's approval of his execution with indifference.

"Chief Warder," he said. "There's only one wish I desire. See that no chaplain is brought to me."

"Don't you believe in God?" asked the Chief Warder.

"I've been striving to be a god for a long time. I'm sure I am by now a god."

On his last day in the condemned cell, the Chief Warder visited him.

"Chief Warder," Obi Chukwu said. "After the Bar Beach show what happens tomorrow, when I am gone?"

The Chief Warder looked at him. He thought Obi Chukwu was wandering whether someone would come for his body after the execution, so that he would not have to lie in an unknown cemetery.

"Don't worry," the Chief Warder said. "Everything is arranged in the way you want it."

"The way I want it. Yes, I know what you think. But what I also want to know is ... where do I go from Bar Beach ... when it is over. I mean ... do you believe there is a life after death. I hear the other condemned men talking about it all the time. What do you think?"

The Chief Warder sighed. He remembered that Obi Chukwu had told him he was sure he was a god.

"The answer Obi Chukwu is in your heart. Go and search it," the Chief Warder said, walking out of the cell.

The following morning the police hustled Obi Chukwu and the other two robbers into a car.

They drove behind police sirens escorted with five cars loaded with anti-riot police.

As soon as they reached Bar Beach, the police led them to a platform and crudely tied them from ankle to neck with ropes.

Obi Chukwu saw the firing squad of six marching onto the field followed by the funeral van. He glanced at other robbers who were shaking with fear. He looked at the three unpolished wooden coffins when the labourers lowered them from the van.

"Have you anything to say?" a police officer asked them.

Obi Chukwu said nothing, he heard the other robbers muttering some words. He also heard the Chaplain urging them to ask for God's forgiveness.

Then the chaplain and the pressmen withdrew from the platform.

The officer gave an order.

The firing squad aimed.

Obi Chukwu saw the crowd melting into a huge monster.

He did not hear the next order from the officer.

CARVING

Osagie, a short man of about sixty with a grey beard and a small face looked at his wife, Amayo, a woman of about fifty with a pretty face who had just brought him his usual breakfast of pounded yam, soup with three pieces of fish and a mug of water.

He looked around the room which had changed very little since he had built it over thirty years ago.

He ate the breakfast in silence, thinking of what had happened in the room. They had brought up seven children all of whom were alive. Three women were married in the town, and the four men were living in different parts of the country. It was only one of the male children who had taken up the occupation of the family: carving statues out of wood.

Osagie looked at his hands and wondered how many statues he had carved out of wood since he started to carve. He remembered the first piece he carved when he was only five years old. It was an elephant; and since then he had never stopped carving.

The voice of his wife turned his thoughts on the devotion she had given him during their thirty years of married life. "It is like the devotion of a mother to her child," he mused. He began to think of doing something for the woman he had dearly loved for thirty years. His thoughts ran at random, but soon he decided to carve out a life-size statue of his wife.

"She is still a pretty woman. Her statue will be beautiful," he said, silently.

He, however, agreed to keep the whole thing a secret from her. When he finished his breakfast, he went to a friend's house where he usually procured pieces of wood for his work. He did not find him at home, but he found his sixteen-year old daughter.

"Belema, I want to have a piece of wood ... big log ... that ebony will do," he said to the girl, pointing to a log of ebony wood.

"What are you going to do with such a log?" Belema asked him in surprise.

"I want to carve a life-size statue. It's very important and urgent," he replied, looking at the girl.

"But you can't carry it. Wait, I'll call my brother, he'll know how to bring it to your workshop," she said.

On his way to the workshop, Osagie's thoughts concentrated for a while on Belema. He remembered she always visited him at his workshop whenever she was returning from the market.

"She's a good girl, very helpful like her father," he said to himself.

When he reached his workshop, at the centre of the town, he sat and pondered on which posture he would carve Amayo's statue. He recalled that he liked his wife best when she knelt down, grinding on a flat stone. So he decided to carve the statue in that posture.

He began the work as soon as the log of wood reached the workshop. He worked gradually, for days, on the statue, aiming to make it a masterpiece.

Sometimes, during the work, he felt like telling his wife, who had never visited the workshop throughout their thirty years of marriage, about the statue, but another part of him would say:

"No, don't tell her. Wait until you have finished it.

Then ask her to come to the workshop and give her a surprise of her life."

He always agreed with that part of himself. But gradually a doubt began to get hold of him.

"Would she be glad? Does she appreciate art work?" he began to ask himself.

She never talked to him about the aesthetic quality of his work, he reminded himself. She regarded it as a means of livelihood, and no more.

"I'll do it because that is the only way I can best show her my appreciation and love for her," another part of him consoled him.

So he continued with the work.

One day, when Osagie had just finished the facial part of the statue, Belema came into the workshop.

"That's really important and urgent. It's the statue of your wife. It's beautiful ... look how you carved the nose and the mouth. It's life-like," she said, looking at the unfinished statue.

Osagie felt exulted.

"Do you think it's really life-like? It's nice to know that a little girl like you can appreciate sculpture. But I don't know whether my wife will like it," he exclaimed, chiselling out.

"Oh for sure! I'm sure she will like it. There's nobody who would not like it. It's really beautiful ... so much like her," she reaffirmed.

"I don't want her to know until I have finished it. So don't tell her please," he said, looking at her.

"Yes, I know you want to surprise her. O.K. I promise, I won't tell her," she responded.

From that day, Belema made a habit of coming to the workshop daily. She came, sat and talked with

89

Osagie until he closed the workshop. He liked her aesthetic appreciation.

Gradually, he became fond of her. Belema did not notice his feelings immediately. She realised his affection later; she in turn fell completely for him.

"I'll carve out your statue as soon as I'm through with this. Maybe yours will be prettier than this," he said to her, when he noticed how jealous she was becoming.

"Then you'll carve out my statue in nude. That will make it more attractive than that one," she replied, pointing to Amayo's statue.

He agreed with the idea though he had never carved out a nude statue.

Osagie began to carve Belema's statue the day he finished his wife's. He also delayed telling his wife about her statue. Belema came daily to the workshop. She took off her clothes and reclined on a mat.

Osagie liked it, and spent more time in the workshop. At home he concentrated his thoughts on Belema's youth and fresh body. Then he began to dislike his wife who noticed, but said nothing.

One Tuesday afternoon after he had finished Belema's statue, a visitor came into his workshop. The visitor looked at the statues.

"The most beautiful piece of sculpture I have ever seen," he said, looking at Amayo's statue. "How marvelous ... it's not only a rare piece of art work but a symbol of Africa. It's great."

Osagie waited anxiously to hear the visitor's remarks on Belema's statue.

"This must be the work of one of those crazy young chaps... Do you train some? No imagination, no beauty, just erotic, nothing beyond the

90

moment of physical experience," the visitor said, looking at Belema's statue.

Osagie felt dizzy.

The visitor turned again to Amayo's statue.

"How beautiful and hard is the face ... you know wrinkles can be beautiful ... is there a living person like this statue or is it your fantasy?" the visitor asked.

The manner in which the visitor talked and gestured in praise of Amayo's statue attracted the passersby. One by one they came into the workshop. When they saw Amayo's statue they all agreed with the visitor's remarks and talked in praise of its beauty. But none talked about Belema's statue.

Soon a crowd gathered in the workshop. In a struggle to see Amayo's statue, Belema's statue was pushed down and broken into pieces.

Osagie closed the workshop very late that day. He walked home, recalling the praises he had heard about his wife's statue which was described as beautiful and life-like by the girl he had begun to love.

EMERGENCY

The ambulance rushed with a siren through the streets, regardless of whether the traffic lights were red, amber or green. It headed to the emergency ward of the hospital, to convey a man who was involved in a ghastly accident. The man, a 36-year-old Nigerian, who had been living and working in London for the past ten years, was returning home from work when a heavy lorry ran over his volkswagen. He was pulled out of the wreckage of his car, conscious, in pain and agony, put on a stretcher, and taken into the ambulance.

During the short journey to the hospital, the siren of the ambulance added greatly to his pain and agony. It was then that Dandam began to remember how, one day, he and his brother transported his father home, when the old man fell down from a tree. They put him on a donkey, led the donkey slowly, asking the old man what they should do to alleviate his agony. One or two times, they stopped the donkey, unloaded the old sick man, like a delicate piece of furniture, under a tree and gave him water.

The sound of the siren cut Dandam's chain of thought. He fell unconscious.

When he regained his consciousness, he looked at the nurse who wore a stern face. He felt terribly thirsty. The sight of the water they gave his sick father came vividly to his mind.

"Yes, water, precious crystal clear water to wet my parched throat," he wanted to ask her.

But then the ambulance blew another siren and Dandam became unconscious again.

"Poor thing, he's terribly smashed. It's impossible

to examine him properly. It looks as if there's internal haemorrhage. He also lost a lot of blood before the ambulance reached the scene of the accident. There's need for transfusion," the doctor said, looking at the figure on the surgical table.

At this moment, Dandam's English wife, Susan, a 27-year-old brunette, heard the news of the accident. She left her child with a neighbour and rushed to the hospital. When she entered the emergency ward she looked pale and could hardly stand on her feet.

The doctor came out and talked to her. "Your husband is seriously hurt. I hope there's no internal injuries. We can't know until we are able to x-ray him."

He then led her to where her husband was lying.

Dandam, who was unconscious since he was brought to the hospital, suddenly stirred, turned his head restlessly on the pillow, moaning a little. He opened his eyes, looked around and thought he was having an electronic nightmare.

"It's all right, darling," she said, softly. "You're quite safe."

Susan told the doctors that she was ready to leave everything in their hands and to abide by their decision. Then her thoughts concentrated on her husband. She remembered the day she had told her parents she was going to marry a black man. They had protested against the very idea. She had done all she could to reason with them, but they had disagreed. However, since she was twenty-two she did not need their consent to marry him and she went on and married Dandam.

And now the man was dying. She thought of

94

loneliness and where to get assistance if her husband were to die. She knew no help would come from her parents.

Dandam looked around the faces around him. Fear gripped him when he saw how fearful they looked at him. Was he being fed into a soulless system, he asked himself silently.

"No, it's impossible. I'm not dying. God allowed me to survive malaria, yellow fever, smallpox and all types of tropical diseases in Nigeria. And now to die in this surrounding," he thought, when he realised he was on a surgical table.

He looked around again. "I'm sick, but they look even sicker. I'm not sharing my pain and agony with them. Why do they look so sick," he marvelled in agony.

His mind went back to how the people in his village looked at his sick father when he was dying. They just looked as if they were looking at the sky. They were not sick because they were looking at a dying man. They looked straight at his face. It made them to think of their own death.

"My mother did not feel the death of my father was horrible. Why do these people think my dying is horrible? Why can't they take it like my people ... that dying is like delivering a child in another way," Dandam wished to tell them.

"Please look at my face. Don't just prolong my life with machines. Remember, I have life and it has to end to manifest itself. So think of my needs," he wanted to beg them.

He felt that their anxiety to prolong his life prevented them from finding his real needs. Did they think he did not want to die? Or did they want him

95

to die to avoid their own death, he asked himself, silently.

"We all must die. The sooner the better," he felt as if to shout at them.

He then remembered his father showed no fear on his face when he was dying.

"Am I showing fear on my face?" he wanted to ask them.

He knew it was true that his father had achieved his goal in life before his death. He had died at the age of sixty-eight. He had brought up all his children. He had many friends. And he had faith.

But he too had achieved his goal in life. Agreed he was thirty-six. And that was no age to die. His child had just started schooling. His wife was young.

Well, he too had had a happy childhood. He had read widely. He had many friends. He had travelled far and wide. Above all he had faith and contentment.

"I have found meaning in my life. So let me die and stop fumbling with me," he felt like telling them.

But would they? He knew even if he had the strength to fight they would not listen to him. They would hold him tightly, sedate him and do all they felt was right to prolong his life without any regard to his opinion or right.

Gradually the pain increased. His vision became blurred and he was once again unconscious.

He was pushed to the x-ray section, where the result revealed no internal injuries. It was, however, found he had cancer.

For days doctors battled to prolong his life. When his condition deteriorated, another x-ray was suggested. It revealed a metastatic tumour in his lung.

His wife was told that he would not live for more than a month. Nobody told Dandam of his condition, but he overheard it when the doctors were discussing it.

Whenever Susan visited her husband, she would smile and keep a good mood. She would talk about the plans they had for themselves and their child.

"Think of our plan to go and settle in Nigeria. It would be marvelous to be where it's always like summer. One can always go to the beach. It must be lovely from the pictures I have seen," she said, not looking at her husband.

About their child she often said:

"He'll feel more at home over there. And the schools aren't that bad. After all you went to school over there and you did very well in your studies here."

Though she knew, deep in her heart, that the chances of her hopes turning to reality were very slim, she refused to face the fact — that her husband was dying — whenever she visited him.

But at home she talked out her fears to the neighbours.

"He's in a hopeless condition. There's very little hope. Doctors say he won't live for more than a month," she explained to them.

She, however, continued to hope for a miracle to save her husband. She read all the medical journals she could lay her hands on, with the hope of finding news of a discovery of a new drug that would cure her husband. She asked people about hospitals

97

where there might be a doctor who could perform miracles.

Dandam felt neither depressed nor angry about his fate. He felt the need to express his feelings to his wife, to tell her of his realisation of the fact that he was dying. He could also see it from the faces of the doctors and nurses.

The vision of what his father did when he realised his fate came to Dandam's mind like a cinema: His father called his three wives, thanked them and pointed out to them that it was not his wish to leave them. It was his creator's. He hoped he would re-marry them in the next world. He prayed that those of them who would like to re-marry after his death would find good husbands.

Turning to his male children, he urged them to take care of their wives, to be law-abiding citizens, to respect old and sick people and to take things in life easy.

He then asked his daughters to love and respect their husbands, to be faithful to them, to love their children and never quarrel with other wives of their husbands.

His father then shared his farms among his male children. He told his family where he should be buried. He expressed all his wishes.

Then he asked the family to forgive him. The family forgave him, and in turn asked the dying man to forgive them. The neighbours also came in, with their children, to ask for forgiveness and forgive a dying man.

"It was time for forgiveness," Dandam mused in agony.

He also remembered that his father took death

98

without any feeling against it or the people around him. His father was neither depressed nor angry about his end.

When the end approached, his father became less talkative. He gestured lightly with his hands. He held the hands of the people who came to visit him. He asked them to sit down near him, then he shook their hands, sometimes holding them for some minutes.

"That's what I want to do," Dandam wanted to say. But he felt the people around him were avoiding him as if he were dying with them.

"Am I death?" he wanted to ask them.

He wanted to tell his wife of his dying wishes. He wanted to see his son, who had never been brought to the hospital since he was admitted, to ask him for forgiveness, to advise him or just to hold his little hands in his dying hand.

He wondered why his friends were not visiting him now. Was it because he was dying that everybody was avoiding him? Did they think they could avoid their own deaths by avoiding a dying man?

What had happened to him last night came vividly to him. He had asked the doctor on duty to forgive him. The doctor looked at him and said:

"You'll be all right. Just take these pills."

Dandam knew the pills were meant to send him to sleep, to avoid pain.

"They always sedate me so that I'll not be in pain," Dandam reflected.

The echo of his mother's advice to his sister on the pain of birth came to his mind with a twinge of pain:

"That pain is a pain after which joy comes, just like the pain of dying."

"Please let me experience the pain and agony of dying like my father," he felt like telling the doctor.

However, a little hope began to dawn in his mind, whenever he was in great pain. He then began to think of the possibility of a miracle to save his life. The hope gradually gained ground in his mind. So when everybody was expecting him to die at any minute, he remained, day after day, in unchanged condition.

He began to respond to the treatment. His external injuries began to heal. The doctors were amazed. They decided to send him for another x-ray. The result showed neither cancer nor metastatic tumour in his lung.

"Incredible," the doctors exclaimed.

"There must be a mistake somewhere," the x-ray technician said.

After an investigation it was found out that Dandam's x-ray photographs were mixed up with those of a patient who had died two weeks ago from a metastatic tumour in the lung.

A STORMY NIGHT

He first saw her sitting on a high stool at the bar sipping a drink. He did not see her full face, only a swell of one cheek. He thought she was twenty. She was wearing a blue dress that clung to the lines of her youthful slim figure.

A man near her touched her shoulder; she turned, giving Wiklund his first clear look.

After that single glance she turned back to her friend. The band started to play *Head or Tail*. Someone from the crowd came and asked her for a dance.

"She is good to watch," Wiklund said to himself. He moved nearer to where she was sitting and ordered a Scotch. He was sipping his second Scotch when she came back. She stood quarter to him so that he had a clear view of her profile. She stood five feet nine, had a small mouth and beautiful teeth.

The band started to play *Strangers in the Night*. Wiklund walked over to her and said, "Would you like to dance?"

"With pleasure," she answered, in a warm husky voice, looking at the tall rather good-looking man who wore horn-rimmed glasses. When they reached the dancing floor, she leaned over to him saying, "What are the chances before the night is through?"

"Very good ones," he responded, smiling. His hands grasped hers and they started to dance. After the dance Wiklund said, "Would you like to have a drink with me?"

"Well, thanks," she replied, holding his hand. They went to the bar, where he ordered drinks. When the drinks came he took one and gave her one saying, "Here is to our meeting." After this he put his glass down. She drank hers with relish, her throat muscles pulling greedily.

"That's good," she said, swinging the glass down. "What's your name?"

"Wiklund, I'm a Swede. What's your name?"

"Bimbo. Is this your first time here?" she asked, crossing her long legs.

"Yes, in fact I came to Lagos two weeks ago," he replied, rubbing his nose with his thumb.

"No girl yet?" she asked, giving him a long look.

"None," he replied, as they moved to a table in a corner.

"I hope I appeal to your sporting instincts," she said, smiling.

"Have you come here alone?" he asked, looking at her face.

"Yes I always do. You did not answer my question," she said, touching his knee.

"You appeal to my sporting instincts," he replied, holding her hand.

"You want to go to bed with me?" she asked.

"I wouldn't mind," he said, tighting his grip on her hand.

"I know you're a newcomer here, but I must tell you I want to be happy tomorrow morning," she murmured, gripping his knee.

"I don't understand," he replied, sipping his drink.

"Well, what I mean is I have to pay a taxi to my house. You may not know things are expensive in Lagos," she said, working her hand on his knee.

Wiklund looked puzzled.

"Would you explain, I really don't understand?" he inquired, lighting her cigarette.

102

"Where do you live?" she asked, puffing the smoke of the cigarette.

"I live in Victoria Island."

"Well, I live at Ikeja. The taxi will charge me about three pounds tomorrow. I paid my ticket to come in. I'm not selling myself, but how much are you going to pay me?"

"I don't know, how much you want?" he asked, lighting his cigarette.

"Would you pay me ten pounds," she said, putting her lips on his chin.

He was silent for a while. She bent forward to pick up a lighter she dropped and he could see she wore no brassiere.

"O.K, I'll pay," he replied, holding her hand.

They came out of the club and took a taxi.

In the taxi she lifted her mouth and Wiklund kissed her. In a quarter of an hour the taxi arrived at a bungalow standing in the centre of well-kept lawns dotted with palm trees.

While she was satisfying her feminine curiosity with sharp penetrating glances into every corner of the room, he put a record on the stereo.

A few seconds later music filtered through the four-wall speaker into the room.

"You want a drink?" he asked, looking at her.

"I do," she replied. He went into the kitchen and returned with two glasses of honey lips.

"Hm, I love this," she said, as he handed her the glass. She put her lips against the glass, kissing it. After sipping it, she put the glass down.

"Get up and dance," she said lazily, kicking off her shoes. "Why don't you come closer," she said, her hands caught his wrists, pulling him to her.

"Where is your toilet," she asked, when the record ended.

A few minutes later she called him and asked him to bring her a cigarette.

When he went he found her standing naked inside the bathroom door.

"Do you want to tell me why I came here?" she asked, holding his hand. "Just to be screwed," she replied herself.

They came back to the bedroom. She undressed him, came to him and kissed him. His arms went around her, drew her closer, kissed her. They fell in the bed.

"Make it to me like a thunderstorm not like a shower," she murmured, as she clung to him.

It was eleven o'clock and a hot morning when Wiklund woke up. He took a cigarette from his bedside table and lit it. He drew the cigarette smoke into his lungs and began to think of his wife. He had written to her only yesterday and told her he had settled in Lagos and that she should come down as soon as possible.

He remembered how he had met his wife, Leena.

It was at a friend's party, after which he drove her to her flat which she was sharing with another girl. He dated her on the way.

One Friday night two months after their first date, they were at his flat when without a word their gaze came back to each other.

"Leena," he said.

"What Wiklund?" she exclaimed, laying her hand on his.

"I love you."

"I love you too, Wiklund " she replied, moving

104

nearer to him. After a few minutes their lips met, gently and lingeringly.

They had married three months later. After two years they had a baby daughter.

One day his boss called him and told him of the urgent need of a man in their sister company in Lagos, but he did not know the right person to send. Wiklund expressed the wish to go.

His wife was glad when he told her of his decision. They then decided that she should remain in Sweden and would come to Nigeria when he settled down.

Wiklund got up from the bed, made coffee and went and took a shower. When he came back to the bedroom he found Bimbo had woken up.

"Good morning," she said, hurrying to the bathroom.

She left immediately after Wiklund had given her the agreed amount, asking, "When shall I see you again?"

"Any time you like," he replied casually.

"The same place?" she asked, as she stepped out of the door.

"Yes," he replied, shutting the door.

After she had gone Wiklund made up his mind not to see her again.

However, in the evening he changed his mind and went to the club. On his way to the club he began to review in his mind the words he would use on Bimbo so that they would never see each other again. But when he saw her outside the club, she came into his arms without hesitation, he then forgot all about words. She kissed him and he felt the blood coming up.

"Shall we go into the club or to your house?" she asked.

"Let's go to my house," he replied, holding her hand.

The taxi driver who had driven them the other time was there.

"Hello, master, you remember me. I was the one who drove you with your friend last time."

They went into the taxi.

"Master, my name is Araba. Whenever you come to club I drive you home. Me alone, I like you," the taxi driver said, as he drove the car towards Victoria Island.

"You like him or you like his money," commented Bimbo.

"Don't tell me master no give you money when you sleep in his house. And you like master too I think. I no use water drive my car. Petrol I use, money I put buy it," he said, putting the car into the third gear.

"I no like im only, I love im," she said, kissing Wiklund.

"Make you go marry im tomorrow," the taxi driver replied.

"We go marry soon," she said.

"You savvy how to cook whitesman's food?" the taxi driver inquired, accelerating the car.

"We fit hire cook," she said. The taxi driver laughed as he negotiated a corner, saying, "I go drive you to registry."

"We go marry in church," she said, putting her palm on Wiklund's chin.

"Then I no go drive you ... me, finish with church. I drive one churchman home one day, but he no give

106

me money. He say he go pray for me. I tell am prayer no make car move," he said, slowing the car.

When they reached Wiklund's house, the taxi driver said: "Make no listen to her, master. Go do what you go pay for ...."

After he had made a drink and they sat down on a sofa, Bimbo said:

"Do you believe in love?"

"I do, but why?" he inquired.

"I don't know," began Bimbo. "I don't understand all those things about love. When I said I loved you in the taxi, I did not feel anything. Is that how love is?" she asked, moving closer to him.

"No, you don't love me," Wiklund replied.

"Oh, I don't mind loving you," she said, putting her arm around his shoulder. "I know I don't come here to be loved but to be screwed. You see, I have no one to look for, no particular type of man in my mind, as the one I'll like to love."

"By the way, how did a clever girl like you get into this fix. Do you do any work?" he asked.

"Work! not for me," she replied, looking straight at him. "Didn't you say I am clever? If you are clever you don't need to work in Lagos. Men work for women in this city."

"Don't you have any hope of marrying?" he inquired.

"I wouldn't mind marrying you," she replied.

"No, you can't marry me. I have a beautiful wife and a daughter," he said, putting his palm on her back.

"Well don't bring your wife to Lagos. Whenever you need a woman, I'll be available," she responded, putting her head on his shoulder.

"You don't believe in marriage?"

"Marriage is not for Lagos. There are plenty of them in the villages. In Lagos there are those that last up to a month or two. Lagos is not a married-couple's city," she said, standing up and gesticulating with her hand.

Wiklund thought she was getting drunk so he got up and put his arms around her, kissing her. She freed herself, saying: "Now you don't want to listen to me, you're getting excited."

He stood examining her critically, saying: "How long have you been in this trade?"

"About three years," she replied straight.

"To come back to our topic about Lagos," she went on. "I'm advising you not to bring your wife here."

"Now look," he said, getting up. "How about going to the bedroom?"

"That's what I'm looking forward to," she responded, picking up her bag.

A few days later Wiklund went back to the night club, looking for Bimbo though he had resolved never to see her again. He did not find her. As usual the taxi driver was there when he left the club at one o-clock.

"Hello my friend, drive me home," Wiklund said to him.

"Your friend no here today?" the taxi driver asked, as he drove the car.

"No I did not see her," Wiklund replied.

"She must be having their usual thing. When they have it they no come to club," the taxi driver said, putting the car into the third gear.

"What is their usual thing?" Wiklund asked.

108

"The thing which every women gets monthly. But Master you fit get another beautiful girl," he said, hooting to the car in front of him.

"No, I prefer her."

"You like am very much."

"Yes."

"But make no marry her. Lagos girls no make good wife," he said, overtaking a car in front of him.

"I'm already married."

"Have you children, Master?"

"A daughter."

"Me four children," the taxi driver said.

"How many wives?"

"Two wives, Master. One wife trouble, two wives no trouble," he said, as he applied the brake.

A week later on a Saturday night, the taxi driver saw Bimbo going into the night club. He called her and told her that Wiklund had come looking for her last week.

"Hey live me alone, I have many friends," she told him.

He grabbed her and said crossly: "You Lagos girls are crazy. You don't remember you even said you love im and you go marry him. The man is my friend, I must look after his interest. Make you go in, but no come out with another man. I go drive you to his house today."

"O.K. I'll go if you go drive me free," she said, trying to free herself from him.

"I agree, but give me your bag, I go hold am."

After she sat down on her usual stool at the bar, a young Nigerian came and asked her for a dance.

"I want a drink before a dance," she told him.

109

"What do you drink?" he asked, smiling.

"Gin and tonic," she replied, smiling. He ordered double gin and tonic for her and bought a coke for himself.

"Are you a company director?" she asked him when she saw the amount of money he was carrying.

"Yes, for an advertising company," he answered.

After they had danced for some minutes he asked her whether she would like to follow him to his house that night.

"Not today," she replied, "I'm waiting for my friend."

"What about if he does not come?" he asked, giving her a cigarette.

"I'll then have to go to his house."

"Are you that serious?" he asked, lighting her cigarette.

"Maybe," she responded, puffing the smoke of the cigarette.

At one o-clock when her friend did not come, he asked her again to go with him.

"In that case you have to pay me here," she said, spreading her palm.

"O.K. I'll pay you in my house."

"This is the usual thing here. If you want me to come with you give me ten pounds," she insisted, still spreading her palm.

He gave her the amount. After some minutes she told him she would like to go to toilet, after which they could go. She did not return, but went out of the club.

"Let's go quick! quick!" she said to the taxi driver, as she got into the car.

"Why, did you thief someone?"

110

"Yes, but it was Lagos man, they too thief us sometimes," she replied, lighting her cigarette. The taxi driver laughed as he accelerated the car.

"It looks as if storm go come soon," he said, as they headed to Victoria Island.

"How do you know?" she inquired.

"You no see the Lagoon no move."

When they reached Wiklund's house it was dead silent. Bimbo went to the bedroom window and knocked, shouting. "Wiklund! Wiklund!"

Leena, Wiklund's wife who had arrived in Lagos the previous day, heard the knocks and shouts before her husband. She woke him up. He got up from the bed followed by her. When he moved aside the window curtain he saw Bimbo.

"You know her. You must have brought her here. How else did she know the bedroom," his wife said, holding him back.

He said nothing.

"I am going to open the door for her and let her in. We must face the truth, Wiklund," she replied, opening the door to let Bimbo in.

When Bimbo realised that it was not Wiklund, she turned back and ran to the taxi.

"Wait! Wait!" she shouted to the taxi, as rain and a gusty wind started.

"Drive me home," she pleaded, wiping out the rain from her face.

"I can't drive now, I no see road," the taxi driver said, switching off the engine.

"Get me out of here," she shouted, hitting him on the back.

"I no savvy grammar," he said, "Ow much you go pay me?"

111

"Two pounds," she replied, searching her bag.

"Get out of my car or pay me ten pounds," he said trying to open the door of the car.

"I fit no pay that."

"Then go out of my car."

"You no pity me."

"Me to sorry you. No be you who don thief someone now, now. Go out of my car or give me ten pounds."

Thunder silenced them.

"O.K. you drive me I go sleep with you," she responded, putting her hand on his back.

"No, I have two wives," he replied, taking her hand away from his back.

"You no like a change?"

"No, I stay with what I have."

"Take! you poor man," she said, giving him the amount.

"Call me what you like I go drive you since you pay me," he said, starting the engine of the car.

Leena and Wiklund went back into the bedroom. He lit a cigarette and smoked in silence for some minutes, then he said.

"I am sorry, Leena."

"Do you love her?" she asked.

"No," he replied.

"Did you bring her here and make love to her?" she inquired.

"Yes..."

"How many times did you make love to her, the first night you brought her?"

"Oh for goodness' sake, why don't you forget about it."

112

"You must tell me all that happened. How many times did you make love to her?"

"Four times," he replied.

"In one night. You did not make that to me on our first honeymoon night."

"Oh, for God's sake Leena."

"Was she good?" she asked.

"She wasn't good," he answered.

"You made love to her four times. You are lying, lying," she screamed, slapping him.

Then their eyes met and locked for a while. Suddenly she threw her arms around her husband saying, "Do it to me more than four times, please. Do it quick please."